Dread Culture

A Rastawoman's Story

by

MASANI MONTAGUE

ISBN 0-920813-53-4

94 95 96 97 98 99 ML 0 9 8 7 6 5 4 3 2 1

Canadian Cataloguing in Publication Data
Montague, Masani
Dread Culture: a Rastawoman's story
ISBN 0-920813-53-4
1. Dread Culture
PS8576.057D7 1994 C813'.54 C93-095238-3
PR9199.3.M65D7 1994

Editors: *Andrea Davis, Honor Ford-Smith,*
   Stephanie Martin, P.K. Murphy
Editor for the Press: *Makeda Silvera*
Production & Design: *Stephanie Martin*
Pre-Production: *Leela Acharya*
Printed and bound in Canada by Metrolitho

Represented in Canada by The Literary Press Group
Distributed by General Publishing

Published with the assistance of the Canada Council and the Ontario Arts Council

Published by:
Sister Vision Press
P.O. Box 217
Station E
Toronto, Ontario
Canada M6H 4E2

In memory of my beloved brother, Clarence

chapter *one*

*A**s a little girl**,* Esther could tell the time of day just by looking at the sky. She believed that roosters possessed this hidden talent too. Each day as the cock's crow signalled a new beginning, she muttered her early morning prayer. "Five o'clock and all is well. Tank God fi anodder day." As the eldest girl child growing up in the Cockpit country with her mother and twelve brothers and sisters, Esther was in charge of the younger ones while her mother and older brothers tended the plot of land next to the house.

The family worked the land, planting enough to feed the family and to sell at the market in the town square. This had been the family's way of life even before she was born. When her father died her mother continued the tradition. While her mother and her older brothers toiled in the sun, Esther and the younger ones tended to the cattle and the few chickens they kept for their own use.

The cock crowed a second time, jolting Esther from her

reverie. "Five thirty and all is well."

As much as she had enjoyed life in the Cockpit country, coming to Kingston had been exciting and challenging for Esther. When Maas Zacharia's son, Emanuel, had proposed marriage and a promising life in the city, she hadn't hesitated to accept. By then, she had already borne him six children. The last three were born shortly after her arrival in Kingston's lower-middle-class Jones Town neighbourhood.

At first, life in Jones Town hadn't been as rewarding as Emanuel had made out it would be and the novelty of living in the city had soon worn off. Esther stayed at home and looked after their nine children, while Emanuel travelled between Kingston and the country, selling clothes and other basic necessities that were scarce in rural areas. They struggled together, working long and hard hours.

Although she missed her country home, Esther had only been able to go back to her village once, and that was for her mother's funeral. How different everything had seemed to her then. Nothing was like she had left it.

Between looking after the children and assisting her husband with his weekly treks, Esther supervised their small but well-stocked haberdashery. She would never have been able to juggle her duties without the help of the six older children.

Once the children were all grown up and had children of their own, Esther and Emanuel retired and began enjoying the rewards they had been pursuing since leaving the serenity of the countryside. Malcolm's Haberdashery was left under the management of the three business-minded offspring. Esther's days were now spent caring for her grandchildren and the six-bedroom house with its big yard and many fruit trees. Her other children were scattered across the world, three in the United States, two in Canada and one in England. The children had often tried to convince their mother to join them abroad, but each time she had replied, "Mi born and grow inna Jamaica and mi gwine dead yah so!" Emanuel, on the other hand, had taken up their son's offer to join him in England. That was some five years ago.

There were times when Esther missed her husband and the rest of her family. Through their letters and frequent telephone calls, she tried to imagine damp, aristocratic England, vast, cold Canada and the romance of the United States of America. But, as much as their tales of far away places excited her, the thought of leaving home for an alien country scared Esther. Besides, who would take care of her grandchildren?

"Wah yuh seh, Granny?" Looking up, Esther saw her granddaughter, Sweetie, staring at her. No, she couldn't leave her grandchildren and everything she had worked to build for the past seventy years to start all over again in a strange land.

"Granny, yuh talking to yuhself again?" Sweetie teased as she went over and hugged the old woman.

"Wah yuh doing up so early? Mi tink is only old people get up when di cock crow," Granny replied. "Unnu young people no know seh unnu mustn mek sun ketch unnu inna bed."

"Cho, das old wives tale, Granny. Yuh mean if we nuh go to bed early and get up early, we nah healthy, wealthy and wise like you?"

"Gwaan mock di ole woman. When me dead and gawn, unnu nah go have nobody fi mock."

"Oh, Granny, nuh chat so. Yuh gwine deh round fi a long time to come. By di way, what yuh was muttering to yuhself bout dis morning?"

"Nutten fi worry yuh head bout. Yuh nah get ready fi school?"

"Granny! Today is Saturday, yuh head not functioning today or what?"

"Gal pickney, mind yuh mout or else mi belt will function pon yuh bottom."

Smiling, Sweetie replied, "Oh Granny, mi nevah mean no disrespect. But yuh mus have a lot pon yuh mind if yuh no memba seh today a Saturday."

"Gwaan yuh ways and no mind what mi have inna mi head. By di way, where is Johnny and Boysie, dem?"

"Dem getting ready fi go down a di shop."

"Good. Yuh Uncle Tanny will need dem fi help him out today. Yuh know how Saturday can busy at di shop. Tell dem fi come and —"

"See dem coming yah, Granny."

"Morning Granny," Johnny addressed the old woman as he came up and kissed her on her cheek.

"Saturday and everyone up bright and early?" Granny exclaimed. "Wah a gwaan?" she asked suspiciously as her third grandchild, Boysie entered the room.

"Nutten fi worry bout, Granny," Boysie answered. "Me and Johnny a go dung di shop fi help out Uncle Tanny and Auntie P today."

"Since when unnu so anxious fi work pon Saturday? Mi

memba days gawn by when unnu used fi give me all sort of excuses why unnu couldn't work at di shop. Now all of a sudden as cock crow, unnu up and ready fi go work. Unnu tink mi born yesterday, eh?"

Sweetie blurted, "Me know why, Granny."

Both Johnny and Boysie glared at her.

"Well, wah unnu up to now?" Granny demanded.

But her grandchildren answered in unison, "Nutten, Granny."

"It better be nutten or else Talawa gwine mek it inna sinting."

The children feared Granny's Talawa, the belt that hung behind the door. On several occasions, they had felt it sting their buttocks. They knew that it was important that Granny not find out anything. Otherwise, all three would be equally punished — Johnny and Boysie for lying, and Sweetie for conspiring with them.

Knowing that her fate was tied to that of her cousins', Sweetie tried to reassure the old woman.

After the children left, Esther swept the yard while Sweetie began preparing the traditional Saturday soup. Sometimes it was hard to put food on the table. Increasingly, Esther worried about the children, especially the boys. Over the years Jones Town had changed. With the coming of armed fighting between rival political gangs and increased unemployment, there was too much trouble for a young man to get into.

Her thoughts went to Johnny. From him born, him no good Puppa nevah give him a penny. What wid di lootin and di shootin pon di one hand, and di police scraping up

9

di youngsters dem pon di corner on di odder, she shook her head. "Lawd, I am asking you to keep watch over him and deliver him from the hands of Satan," she prayed. She continued sweeping as she hummed her favourite spiritual.

Boysie and Johnny closed the gate behind them and strolled down Benbow Street. Usually they would stop and chat with their friends hanging out on the corner, but not even the thought of winning some money on the crown-and-anchor board or in a card game could lure the cousins from their destination today. As they passed the crowd, a boy shouted, "Wah appen, Johnny, Boysie, weh di action deh?"

"Wah appen, Chuckie! No action! Jus a pass through," Johnny said.

"Come try yuh luck pon di board, man. Ah feel today is yuh lucky day," called Chuckie, the neighbourhood crown-and-anchor man.

"Not today, man. We deh pon a mission," Boysie added.

"Wah! Business a gwaan pon Benbow Street and me no inna it? Since when money a mek and mi nah get a piece of di action? Unnu forget who control di action round yah?"

"Relax Chuckie, man. A nuh money mission. A different kind of runnings, man. Nutten yuh would be interested in," Johnny replied.

"Cho! From money nuh involve, den a nuh nutten of importance. A pickney business den." With that, Chuckie returned to the game, his conversation with Johnny and Boysie at an end. "See di crown and anchor man, yah. Try yuh luck today," he shouted as the cousins continued their stroll along Benbow Street.

As they reached Price Street where their Uncle Tanny's shop was located, they saw Sala, a school friend and confidant. Sala was talking to Pinky, one of the go-go dancers who worked in his mother's bar, the Blue Jug. He was so caught up in the conversation with the stripper that he didn't hear Johnny and Boysie as they came up.

"Wah appen Sala, yuh nuh fraid she strain yuh? Mind yuh nah tek on more dan yuh can manage," Boysie teased.

Sala looked slightly embarrassed. "Hey! Yuh cyaan sneak up pon people dem way deh. Wah yuh a run off yuh mout seh, Boysie?"

"Mi seh fi stop tek up more dan yuh can manage, man," Boysie snickered. "Yuh a lickle bwoy a try do a man's job."

"Tell dem seh me a man enough fi yuh, nuh dahling."

Pinky laughed loudly and replied, "Mi will talk to yuh bwoys later. Mi have work inside fi do."

"Hey Pinky, Pinky Tell dem nuh!" Sala called out as she retreated into the bar. Pretending to be hurt, he protested, "Cho! A true she nuh want nobody fi know we business, man. But a long time she in love wid me, yuh know. So, we all set fi go pon dis mission?"

The three boys arrived at the haberdashery store to find their Uncle Butty loading boxes onto his truck and were told by Uncle Tanny that they would be helping his brother on the truck that day instead of working in the store. Turning to Sala, Johnny whispered, "It nuh look like we can go pon di mission wid yuh today, Sala."

"What? Look how long we a plan dis trip yah. You

11

know how hard it was to convince Joe Man to tek us wid him to di celebration? Cho!"

"Listen, man, yuh know seh we did a look forward to dis day, right?" Sala didn't respond. "Well, yuh hear Uncle Tanny just now. If we was working in di shop den it would be easier to sneak off early. Once we start work wid Uncle Butty pon him delivery yuh know seh him a go end up inna Allman Town."

"But why dis Saturday of all days?"

"We feel just as bad as you, man, but we nuh have no choice. If we nuh go wid Uncle Butty, him gwine tell Granny and yuh know how dat go. She suspicious already as it is. Maybe is good dat tings no work out. Yuh know how she feel bout Rastafari."

"A dat time she would a kill us." Boysie was remembering Talawa.

As the boys talked, their uncle, a short, stocky man with a receding hairline came up to them. Although he was in his mid-thirties, Tanny gave the impression of a man who had seen more years. When his parents had decided to put the reins of the family business in their children's hands, he hadn't realized that he would have to take on so much responsibility.

At first, picking up where his parents had left off had been relatively easy, but as the years passed, maintaining the business became an increasing challenge. The rising crime rate in Western Kingston — the store along with other stores in the area had been robbed several times — made it hard, and the rising cost of living put pressure on sales, but most important was Butty's decision to branch out on his own in Allman Town.

Tanny could cope with the other problems, but Butty's decision was a harsh blow. Some family members supported the decision, but others called it selfish, a deliberate move to destroy the links forged by their parents. At the same time, his sister Madge, though committed to the family business, found that the demands of her husband and children limited the time she could spend in the store. Tanny was left with the task of keeping Malcolm's Haberdashery alive in Jones Town.

In spite of their differences, Tanny and Butty maintained a cordial business relationship, and when Butty asked Johnny and Boysie to help him with his delivery, Tanny readily agreed because he knew his brother would later loan the truck to the store.

Looking at his younger brother sitting behind the steering wheel, Tanny admired his determination, although he would never admit it out loud. "Time fi go, bwoys." Walking toward the driver's door, he added, "So yuh all set now, Butty?"

"Yeah, it look so. Me jus have fi mek one more stop pon Slipe Pen Road before me reach Allman Town."

"Yuh a stop a di Chineyman shop fi di rest of di goods?"

"Yeah, might as well. Me will see yuh lickle more," Butty added as he clasped his elder brother's hand.

Turning to Johnny and Boysie, who by then were sitting on boxes stacked in the truck, Tanny called out, "Unnu bwoys nuh give yuh uncle no trouble now, yuh hear? Else ah will mek him buss unnu ass." Both boys grinned. "Unnu tink unnu too big fi get beating, don't it?"

13

Lowering his voice slightly, Tanny turned to Sala. "So how is yuh madda, young man?"

"Fine, sah. Just fine." Sala smiled. Tanny's affection for the Blue Jug's proprietor was no secret to most of the people of Price Street. His wife, Polly didn't know. A staunch Christian, Polly regarded the bar's owner and her strippers as sent to lead God-fearing men into sin.

"Tell yuh madda dat me seh fi tell her hello," Tanny added as he went back into the shop.

As they helped Uncle Butty unload the truck, a Rastaman walked up, greeting them, "Rasta love, Brother Butty. Peace, youthman."

"One love, Iyah Nyah," Uncle Butty responded.

"One love," the cousins echoed in unison. Last year they had met Iyah Nyah in Allman Town. Since then they had longed to know more about Rastafari and the people who spoke so confidently about their religion and way of life. They had come to know the Rastaman through their Uncle Butty when the Rastafarian had come to buy lumber from the store and had stared in awe as he conversed with Butty outside the shop. As he left, Iyah Nyah had said to them, "Peace and love, youthman. Rastafari liveth!" Too shy to answer, they had only grinned as he walked away. Uncle Butty had put his arms around their shoulders as they headed back into the store, and although he hadn't said anything, they had gotten the impression that Uncle Butty had a very deep respect for the Rastaman. It was then they decided that Uncle Butty was their favourite uncle. They had not seen Iyah Nyah since then.

Gathering his courage, Johnny blurted out, "Yuh going to di Nyah Binghi celebration?"

Iyah Nyah looked at him and smiled. "What di I know about di Nyah Binghi celebration?"

"Nutten," said Boysie. Encouraged by Johnny's boldness, he continued, "But we would like to know something about Rastafari."

Obviously surprised by the boys' revelation, Iyah Nyah replied, "Yeah, I man a trod to di Nyah Binghi celebration inna Bull Bay now."

"Really!" Johnny exclaimed. "Could we go, Uncle Butty?"

"Yes, Uncle Butty, could we go?" Boysie pressed.

Iyah Nyah cut in, "Nyah Binghi is a serious ting, youthman. Maybe is better if di youthman dem wait lickle before dem go. Rastafari liveth forever so di I dem have nuff more time to trod. Brother Butty, I man a trod dung di road now."

Butty looked at his nephews' disappointed faces and felt himself giving in. Although he had never locksed his hair, he had always maintained that he had Rastafari in his heart. He understood his nephews' wish to learn more about the Rastafarian religion, but he also knew that their grandmother would be very angry if she found out that he had allowed them to go. His mother's views reflected the wider community's contempt and intolerance of the Rastafari Movement and its followers. That the Movement openly extolled the use of ganja created even more tension between the Movement and "Babylon."

In 1927, Marcus Garvey had prophesied, "Look toward

Afrika when a black king shall be crowned, because the day of deliverance is near." Since then the Rastafari Movement had been an irritant to the "respectable" Jamaican community. Butty vividly recalled Emperor Haile Selassie I's visit to Jamaica in 1966. He and his best friend had skipped school that day to go to the airport to watch the arrival of the King of Kings, Lord of Lords, Conquering Lion of the Tribe of Judah. That was a day he would never forget. Pandimonium broke out when the plane landed and he had been able to catch only a brief glimpse of the Emperor's smile through the thick crowd. He would never forget that face as long as he lived.

Looking at his two nephews now, Butty was proud of their interest in Rastafari though he would never admit this to his mother. Butty signalled to the Rasta man that he wanted to speak to him in private. They were gone for only a few minutes, but to the boys it seemed like hours. Finally, the two reappeared. "Okay bwoys, unnu have mi permission to go wid Iyah Nyah. Him give mi him word dat everything gwine be alright." Coming closer to the boys, he added, "Of course dis is between you and me, now."

Johnny and Boysie trudged behind Iyah Nyah along the long, rocky road leading to the Nyah Binghi camp. Their hearts beat rapidly as the heavy rhythmic beat of the drum got louder. As they entered the assembly, several Rasta brethren and sistren hailed Iyah Nyah. It seemed like nobody noticed them, but the boys felt deeply honoured to be a part of the group. They stood spellbound as several members of the congregation danced around the tabernacle.

Then, as worshippers tossed more wood into the fire burning outside, a loud burst issued from the flames. "Jah Rastafari!" someone shouted in reverence, and the words of praise were echoed by the group, "Jah Rastafari!"

The cousins' hearts raced. They couldn't wait to brag to Sala and the rest of the gang.

chapter two

The sound of bells and the loud chanting of the crowd broke the silence of the classroom as the Party supporters strode along Spanish Town Road toward Denham Town Secondary School. As the crowd reached the school, at the corner of North Street and Spanish Town Road, the noise grew louder. The bickering and screaming of several voices could be heard above the rest. Johnny and most of his classmates strained to hear what was brewing at the rally. Mr. Smith, the history teacher, commenced his speech on Christopher Columbus' escapades in the Caribbean, oblivious, as usual, to his students.

The bell sounded and springing from their seats, Johnny, Boysie and Sala raced from the classroom and toward the rally. In the distance, a police siren wailed. The boys reached the crowd just as a police car pulled up. Getting out of the car, a policeman strutted toward the crowd and demanded, "Wah a gwaan?"

A bystander answered, "A school bwoy attack a woman

and — see di woman over deh, officer, sah!" He abruptly pointed to a woman surrounded by onlookers.

Going toward the woman, the policeman asked her, "Wah appen to yuh, madda?"

The bystander, following closely behind the policeman, replied, "A school bwoy attack her and — "

The policeman glared at him. "Wait now. Since when yuh start wear frock? Shut yuh mout and mek di woman talk!" Passersby snickered as the man sulked. Ignoring him, the policeman went on. "Yes, madda, yuh was saying?"

Dabbing at her eyes, the old woman sobbed. "Mi was marching dung Spanish Town Road wid di others when mi feel someone pull mi bag from under mi arm. By di time mi turn round di bwoy tek off wid mi bag wid all mi lickle savings inna it."

Taking out his notebook and pen, the policeman asked, "Did yuh get a good look pon him?"

The bystander had kept quiet for a while, but now he spoke. "See one of di tiefin bwoy dem deh, officer."

"Who ask yuh anyting? How come yuh know so much? Yuh sure is not you who steal di woman money?"

The man pulled in his stomach and stood very straight. "Officer, sah, me is a born-and-bred Christian who nevah tief a penny from mi born."

"So how come yuh know so much bout dis incident?"

"Mi was just passing by when mi hear di woman a bawl out fi tief, and mi start fi run after di bwoy, but mi bad foot start hurt me. Officer, sah, from mi start mek two shillings di people inna di yard obeah mi and give mi bad foot. Yuh see how nayga people bad-minded and grudgeful?"

"Stop chat foolishness bout obeah and tell us wah appen to di woman and she money."

Looking around the crowd, the man spotted Johnny and his friends, who, like the others, stood listening. Grabbing Sala, he pushed the terrified boy toward the officer and shouted, "See di tiefin bwoy yah so, officer."

"No! Ah nuh me sah."

"Shut yuh mout and get inna di car."

"But officer, sah, me and mi friends dem just a come from school — "

"All unnu school bwoy a tief. Unnu won't stop preying pon innocent people."

"But officer, sah, we jus a come from school — " Johnny cut in.

"Yuh want to join yuh friend in di back seat?"

"No sah, no sah!"

"Well, mind yuh blasted business den."

He jumped into his car and sped away, dust flying in all directions. Johnny and Boysie looked at Sala helplessly as the car turned the corner. They walked away, not quite believing what had happened. As the crowd recounted the incident, some people rejoiced that the policeman had finally caught up with one of the culprits plaguing the community, while others argued that an innocent boy had just been taken away.

Johnny and Boysie walked home in silence. The incident shook them. They knew that it could have been either of them instead of Sala, and they would never forget that frightened look on Sala's face.

The cousins were so caught up in their thoughts that

they didn't realize they had reached Benbow Street until they heard Chuckie bellowing, "See di crown-and-anchor man yah! Try yuh luck today." Spotting the cousins, Chuckie called out, "Wah appen, Johnny? Boysie? What a way unnu look like unnu see duppy."

"Yuh waan see di police dem jus arrest Sala."

"Fi wah? Weh him do?" Chuckie asked, amused.

"Chuckie, dis is not a laughing matter," Johnny replied angrily.

Boysie began with the sound of the crowd, and as he continued, the smile slowly faded from Chuckie's face. Other boys on the corner listened and lamented Sala's plight but wished they had shared in the adventure. Leaving them to debate what each would have done had he been in Sala's position, the cousins continued home along Benbow Street.

Sweetie and a group of children from the neighbourhood were playing dandy-shandy in the yard. Granny sat on the verandah in her rocking chair. Squinting, she peered at the letter in her hand. Rubbing her eyes, she called out, "Sweetie, come read dis letter what yuh Auntie Doris send me. Mi eyes not as good as dem use to be."

"But Granny, me is di last one lef inna di game, so mi haffi go to ten."

"Listen, gal pickney, nuh give me no backchat. If yuh nuh come read dis letter fi mi, yuh nah live fi finish di game," Granny threatened.

Immediately, Sweetie left her friends and went to sit on the verandah with her grandmother. Taking the letter from her, she began, "My dear Mama, I hope my letter finds you

in the best of health. Everybody here is fine. My prayers
have finally been answered. I have just received a letter from
the Canadian immigration department telling me that Johnny
was granted his permanent stay in Toronto. I will — "

"Tanks be to Jesus, tanks be to God!" Granny interrupted.

"Granny, di letter nuh finish yet."

"Yuh hear dat, Sweetie? Yuh cousin goin to foreign."

"Dere is more, Granny."

"Hurry up and finish di letter. Unnu young people tek
all day fi do something." Spotting Johnny and Boysie opening the gate, she called out, "Johnny, come yah bwoy
pickney. Yuh goin to foreign, bwoy."

"Wah?"

"Yuh deaf, bwoy? Mi seh yuh a go a foreign to yuh
madda. Sweetie, read di letter again fi Johnny."

"My dear Mama, I hope my letter finds you — "
Sweetie began again.

"Not dat part of di letter. Unnu pickney can't do nutten
right. Here, Johnny, read di letter fi yuhself."

Johnny stared at his feet. "Wah do yuh bwoy? Today
should be di happiest day of yuh life and yuh look like a
poor ting pickney. Yuh nuh happy fi go a Toronto to yuh
madda?"

"Yes, Granny."

"Well look happy and stop look like smaddy dead fi
yuh. Johnny, yuh nuh look yuhself. Wah do yuh?"

"Di police dem just lock up Sala," Johnny blurted out.

Granny raised her eyebrows. "Fi wah? Weh him do?"

"Nutten Granny. Me, him and Boysie a come from

school when we see a crowd a people round dis woman. As we reach up to dem, di police car pull up. Dis man tell di police dat a Sala tief di woman bag wid money."

"Yuh nevah tell di police dat a nuh so it happen?"

"Granny, dem almost arrest me too. As a matter of fact, it could a be either me or Boysie lock up now inna prison."

"Lawd have mercy pon us! How mi would a manage? Dat would a send mi to mi grave sooner dan di good Lawd ready fi me." Granny dabbed her eyes. "What dis country coming to?"

Norman Manley Airport was brimming with people. Mothers dashed after toddlers who rushed past tourists clasping luggage they feared had been lost. Older children were left fidgeting atop piles of boxes and suitcases. Grandmothers cautioned. Small boys punched each other on the arms, acting tough in front of their older brothers. Johnny's family and friends had come out to say goodbye. Some of them wished that they were the ones leaving while others were just glad for Johnny's good fortune. They laughed about Johnny's adventures, raising their voices against the noise of aeroplane engines filling the background.

"Memba di time when Johnny was asleep wid him mout open and Sweetie put a piece of paper in him mout?" Boysie teased.

"Yeah, but a yuh light di paper."

"Yuh should a see yuh face when di fire reach yuh mout. Yuh get up and run like duppy a chase yuh."

"Memba one night when Sweetie go tell Granny dat Rolling Calf follow her home?" Johnny and the others laughed.

"Sweetie, yuh should a see yuh face." Boysie pointed at her.

"Gweh. Mi did know seh a yuh and Johnny a trick me."

"Den why yuh run inna di house and bawl out, 'Granny, Granny, duppy after me'?" Johnny laughed.

The announcer's voice cut into the laughter. "All passengers for Flight 993 leaving for Toronto, Canada, please board the aircraft now."

Granny motioned towards the departure gate. "Johnny, das yuh plane. Hurry up before it leave yuh."

"But Granny, if a fi him plane, it cyaan leave him."

"See yah, bwoy pickney, nuh bodder wid yuh facetiness or else mi gwine give yuh a backsiding right yah in di airport. Talawa might nuh deh yah, but mi hand dem still strong."

"Sorry, Granny," Boysie grinned sheepishly.

"Now, Johnny, memba fi behave yuhself in Toronto. Don't give yuh madda no trouble. She go tru a lot to get yuh up to Toronto. She seh Canada is a nice place wid plenty opportunity fi one fi better demself. So mek good use of dat opportunity."

"Last call for Flight 993 leaving for Toronto," the announcer's voice boomed over the intercom.

"Johnny, hurry up before di plane leave yuh. Give yuh Granny a kiss. And memba fi write as soon as yuh reach," Granny said.

"Yes, Granny. Bye Granny, bye Sweetie, bye Boysie, bye everyone. Mi promise fi write everybody," Johnny yelled as he ran toward the departure gate, his friends and relatives still waving at him.

Granny let out a sigh as she saw the airplane bound for Toronto take off. Oh God, she prayed to herself, tank yuh fi answering mi prayers. Only you know how much mi worry bout Johnny getting inna trouble. Only last month Miss May's son was arrested by di police fi someting him nevah do. Johnny is a good bwoy, but yuh know how di youth dem always get inna trouble. Him finally safe now dat him gone to Canada.

Johnny timidly sat in the seat he'd been directed to by the flight attendant. He was dressed in a new outfit his mother had sent for the occasion. His new shoes pinched his feet, but he hadn't dared refuse to put them on when Granny handed them to him. As soon as he reached his mother's house he was going to kick them off. Apart from visiting Bull Bay, he had never ventured outside of Kingston. The very thought of going to a different country scared him, but he was also gripped by the idea of meeting new friends and seeing his mother and her family. He looked at the new watch Uncle Butty had given him. Only four o'clock. Bwoy, it feels like four years since mi leave Yard. Ah wonder wah Boysie and Sweetie doing now. Who Granny a go give mi bed to now dat mi gone? Granny, mi miss yuh so much. Wah mi a go do without yuh? He drifted off to sleep.

"First love, right?" A finger poked him in the arm.

Johnny struggled to open his eyes. For a second he forgot that he was on a flight bound for Toronto, and then he noticed the woman in the next seat staring at him.

"Dat was some dream yuh was having. What she like?"

"Why yuh tink is a girl mi was dreaming bout?"

"Is di send off present she give yuh last night mek yuh smile so?"

Blushing at the woman's directness, Johnny tried to change the subject. "So tell me, Toronto nice?"

"Oh, yuh nuh want fi talk bout it. Das all right. Toronto have its problems but is a nice place fi live."

"Wah kind of problems?"

"All kine a racism, fi one. Last month a white man shoot down a Jamaican youth fi nutten. According to di man, di first Black person him see, him a go kill. Dis youth was coming from work and di white man shoot him down in cold blood."

"Him should a get life sentence fi dat."

"All dem gwine do is send him to di mental hospital 'cause dem have him down as a madman already. Him shoot di youth 'cause him seh him tired fi see all di white girls dating Black guys."

"Bwoy, Toronto dread."

"It nuh so bad like New York, though. Yuh can still find a good place fi live and a half-decent job if dat is wah yuh want. But mi nuh — but stop, nuh bad bwoy Rankin dat?"

She pointed down the aisle to a flashily dressed Jamaican man returning to his seat. His many gold chains and gold tooth shone brightly as the lights bounced off them.

"Rankin? Di bwoy dat shoot down nuff man last month?"

"Him same one. It look like di Party a send him to Toronto fi cool him out."

"Me nuh like dem kind a bwoy. Dem kill too much

innocent people. Dem — "

The pilot's voice cut in over the intercom: "We'll be landing in Toronto in the next few minutes. Please remain in your seats and fasten your seatbelts. Flight attendants, please prepare for landing."

Through the window, Johnny peered at night-time Toronto. What beautiful lights. Mi finally gwine see mi madda. Ah wonder wah she look like? Ah wonder if she memba me? What if her family nuh like me? Oh Granny, if only yuh was here. The cheers of other passengers broke into his thoughts as the airplane landed on the runway.

chapter *three*

The tired passengers filed out of the airplane and headed toward Immigration. With travel documents in hand, Johnny waited nervously in line. Rankin stood confidently in the next queue. Johnny peered around as some passengers were sent to see another Immigration officer while others were allowed to go and collect their luggage. Man, what a lot of white people. Not even one Black person working at di desk.

"Mr. Smith, who will you be staying with in Toronto?" the Immigration officer asked.

"Mi madda, sah."

"What kind of work does your mother do?"

Johnny hesitated. "Ah tink she is a nurse."

"You don't know what kind of work your mother does?"

Flustered, Johnny mumbled, "Sah, I haven't seen mi madda in twelve years and mi grandmadda is di one dat writes to her."

"What will you be doing in Toronto?"

"Ah guess mi will be goin to school."

Scowling at Johnny, the officer scribbled on a piece of paper and handed it to him, along with his passport. Johnny walked away, feeling a bit confused. Had he said or done something wrong? As he left the desk, another officer looked at the paper and signalled for him to go to another section.

Entering the room, he saw some of the passengers from his flight. All were Black. Standing next to another Jamaican, he could hear voices coming from a cubicle.

" You say your name is Maggie Leah Samuels, but here in your passport you have Margarette Lee Samuels. Besides, the date of birth you have in your passport doesn't match the one on your birth certificate."

Protesting, the woman began, "Dere was a mix-up wid mi birth certificate. Yuh see, I was born on di 29th of June, 1945, but because we was living in di country mi madda didn't get to register mi till di 2nd of July. In regards to mi name, it was di girl in di registrar's office dat spell di names wrong. I have tried several times to get dis clear up and — "

"I'm sorry, Miss Samuels. There's no way I can be sure that the Maggie Leah Samuels born the 29th of June, 1945, is the same person as the Margarette Lee Samuels who's registered on the 2nd of July, 1945. What kind of work do you do in Jamaica?"

"I sell clothes on di sidewalk."

"How can you afford to take a three-week vacation on what you make from selling clothes on the sidewalk?"

"Mi sister buy di plane ticket. Ah only provide di spending money. She will look after me in Toronto."

"If you were to get a job in Toronto would you take it?"

"Well, sah, ah might consider it, seeing dat di clothes business get so slow."

A few minutes later the woman came out of the cubicle, accompanied by a guard. Turning to the Jamaican man standing next to him, Johnny asked, "Why dem taking dat woman away?"

"Dem probably put her pon a bond and she gwine go fi a hearing before dem release her."

"Johnny Smith," called an Immigration officer.

Walking hurriedly, Johnny reached the counter. The man behind the counter looked through Johnny's documents, then said, "You don't seem to know much about your mother. But that's par for the course I guess, with you people. Go on."

Outside in the arrival area, relatives and friends waited impatiently for the passengers from Flight 993. "Dem a come out now," Sandra, leader of the Golden Girls Posse announced as she watched passengers from Jamaica pick up their suitcases and move toward Customs. As if she had given a signal, the crowd surged forward, everyone hoping to catch a glimpse of a loved one or friend. Those at the front braced their hands against the glass partition in order to ease the pressure from behind. Next to Sandra, a woman blew kisses through the partition at her boyfriend.

Standing just close enough to see the passengers was a tall, immaculately dressed man in a three-piece suit with matching hat. He slid his dark glasses down his nose to survey the arrivals. Throughout the years, he had trained himself to study his surroundings even when he wasn't working.

As he examined the crowd he recognized a few regular faces from Toronto. As usual, loud-mouth Sandra and her posse were making a lot of noise. None of them worked, depending instead on shop-lifting and the break-and-enterings of their boyfriends to support their expensive taste in clothes and jewellery.

The man smiled broadly as he recognized a modestly dressed Rastafarian woman in the crowd. He tilted his hat slightly, straightened his tie and sauntered toward Sheba. She smiled politely as he came up to her. "Of all di people mi haffi meet at di airport. Mi hope him nuh come and start run off him mout," she muttered to herself.

"Wah appen, Sistah Sheba?" Spider looked her up and down.

"Wah a gwaan, Spider? Yuh come to meet somebody from Yard?"

"Yeah man, one of mi carriers."

"Business as usual, eh?"

"Yuh know how it go. Part of di survival game. So who yuh meeting? Yuh king man?"

"No, mi lickle bredda, Johnny. Him a come live wid us in Toronto. A di first time in five years mi a go see him."

"Das how long yuh live in Toronto?"

"Yeah, man. Five long years."

"Yuh nevah forward a Yard from yuh come a T.O.?"

"Ah cyaan afford it. So when was di last time yuh go home?"

"Bout last week. Jamaica nice as usual. Mi trod deh at least three times a year."

"I'm a poor student. Wid fi yuh business, yuh can afford anyting."

"Just say di word and yuh'll be in Jamaica tomorrow."

"Wait, yuh waan me fi turn one a yuh carriers?"

"Come on, Sistah Sheba, yuh know me wouldn't check yuh as a mule. Dat is fi posse girls like Sandra and her friends. Yuh more decent dan dat."

"Wah bout yuh mules, as yuh call dem? Dem nuh deserve no better? What if dem get busted? Don't yuh care?"

"Me care bout all mi mules and ah tek care of all dem needs. If you allow me, all your needs could be taken care of too."

"Really." Sheba walked away, leaving Spider snickering.

One of his mules tried to catch his eye. He stared past her but tensed as he watched her walk toward another officer and more questioning. She emerged a few minutes later and joined the other passengers at the luggage carousel.

The passengers smiled broadly as they recognized the people waiting for them. Skimpily dressed Canadian tourists mingled with primly dressed Caribbean grandmothers. Spider's mule was dressed like a paid model.

"Rahtid," said Sandra, chuckling. "Look pon dat one. She certainly dress fi kill. Ah wonder which man she a eat out?"

"As long as is not any a fi mi man dem, dat okay," one of Sandra's posse retorted.

"Look pon dat woman, she nuh realize seh crinoline outta style," another added.

"She probably have dat dress put up inna her bed trunk fi years, waiting fi di day when she would a come a foreign," a third posse member cut in.

The woman standing next to Sandra guffawed and asked, "Ah wonder if dat was how mi did look when mi first come yah? Look pon di man face how it favour cow under shade."

Pointing to a woman in an old-fashioned dress, a man standing nearby joined in, "Ku heng-pon-nail, eh?"

"Lef di woman, man. Yuh nuh see seh she come from country," a fourth posse member said heatedly.

At that moment, Johnny moved toward the luggage circling on the carousel.

"Look pon dat lickle bwoy pickney. Why dem cut off him hair so? It look like peel head John Crow," Sandra said.

"Hey, wait a minute, das mi bredda yuh talking bout," Sheba said.

"Is yuh bredda? Have mi apology." Sandra looked contrite.

Sheba banged on the glass partition to attract Johnny's attention.

"Yuh bredda cute, though," Sandra teased.

"Lef mi bredda alone. Him only seventeen years old," Sheba replied, waving at Johnny.

"Das okay, mi will train him."

"Yuh stay deh a check out man, yuh waan Rankin bus yuh ass?" one of the posse members put in.

"Talking bout Rankin, how come we nuh see yuh man yet? Yuh sure is dis flight him a come pon?"

"Dat is what him seh di last time him call me," Sandra said.

"Yuh sure him coming? Suppose him decide to stay wid him babymadda?"

"Him nuh have no choice. Di Party a send him abroad because of di big shootout last month. Him get too hot fi dem fi handle back home. Him nuh suppose fi have no problem wid di false documents dem give him."

"But stop, nuh Rankin dat a come now? Him look boasty nuh rass," Sandra said as she saw her boyfriend leaving the Immigration area.

Rankin, one of Jamaica's well-known and most wanted gunmen, was strolling toward the line of passengers heading for Customs. He smiled confidently as Sandra and her friends banged excitedly on the glass partition.

"Lawd missis, stop di noise inna mi head. How yuh expect him fi hear yuh through di glass?" a woman standing next to them declared. Ignoring her, they banged even harder.

Inside the baggage clearance area the travellers waited impatiently, hoping to spot their suitcases among the hundreds of bags moving on the conveyor belt.

"Ketch dat red one fi mi, youthman," the woman who had sat next to Johnny on the airplane said, pointing to a heavy-looking suitcase.

"See it yah." Johnny grabbed the suitcase and handed it to her. "What yuh have in it so heavy? Gold?"

"Almost."

"Ah hope di Customs people dem no bodder keep us up all night till dem check everyone."

"A nuh everybody dem check, it's only us Jamaicans. Look how dem let all di Canadians pass through without blinking a eye pon dem. We Yardie will haffi stay all night if it please dem."

"But why?"

"Wah appen to dis youth, eeh? A di first yuh travelling?"

"Yeah. Mi coming to live wid mi madda and her family," Johnny answered.

"No wonder yuh ask a fool-fool question like dat. Mi travel at least seven times a year and every time mi come up mi haffi go through dis. Is only when di plane from Jamaica come up dat yuh see so many Customs people working, yuh know. Look deh now, yuh see dat white Canadian girl and di Jamaican man walking together? Look wah a go appen."

"Dem gwine let di Canadian girl go through but stop di Jamaican man?"

"Yuh nuh see nutten yet. Ah bet yuh dem search at least three-quarter if not all of us."

"Why dem a dig dung dat woman suitcase so?"

"Dem a look fi ganja."

"Is dat why dem a search all di Jamaicans so? Mi know nuff people who get busted tekkin di chance of carrying herb from Yard, but mi nah do it."

"Fi every one dat get busted yuh have three dat get weh. Right now, is di only way me see Black people can mek a decent money inna dis country."

"Dat is not di only way. Mi madda not doing it and she all right. She works in a hospital and mi stepfaada owns a restaurant," Johnny said proudly.

"Weh yuh madda deh now?"

"At work, das why mi sister come fi meet me."

"Ah. She have fi slave all night when she should be meeting her son who she nuh see dis long time. Youthman,

35

yuh have a lot to learn. Di jobs dat most Blacks have yah pay pittance. Di few dat have a decent job haffi wuk damn hard fi keep it. Your stepfaada must be one of the lucky ones. Mi rather try beat di system because mi know dat if mi succeed, mi is at least several tousand dollars richer."

"An if yuh nuh succeed and dem ketch yuh?"

"Das part of di game. Yuh win or lose."

"Yuh carrying up any herbs now?"

"She dat keepeth her tongue keepeth her freedom."

"Smart girl." Johnny cleared his throat. "By di way, I'm Johnny. You?"

"Heather."

"You have any bwoyfren?"

"Wah appen to dis pip-squeak? Yuh know mi could be yuh madda?"

"No, man, maybe mi big sistah but not mi madda." He flushed, feeling he had really flattered her now.

The woman laughed loudly, "How many youth yuh tink me have?"

"Yuh have youth? Yuh barely look sixteen."

"Sweet mout. Yuh gwine give all di girls in Toronto heartache wid a mout like dat."

"Dem nuh have nutten fi fear, man, Johnny-Lover can cure any aches and pain."

"Is a pity ah not ten years younger." Heather had now reached the head of the line. "Youthman, now is mi time. Ah hope everyting okay. Nice chatting wid you." She took a deep breath and pushed her trolley forward.

Spider tensed as Heather moved toward Customs. During her conversation with Johnny, Spider had watched with amusement. Now that she was going through Customs, he felt uneasy and he jumped as Sheba asked, "She come out yet?"

"Uh? Oh a you, Sheba. Mi nevah see yuh come up. Mine dem jim skreechie business deh, yuh know."

"What jim skreechie business? Everyting all right?"

"Sure. Who yuh seh was yuh man?" Spider added quickly.

"Mi nevah seh."

"Well?"

"Well wah?"

"Who is yuh man?"

"Nobody yuh know."

"Don't be so sure. I know practically every herbsman in Toronto."

"Why yuh tink him is a herbsman? Yuh tink selling ganja is di most important ting in life, eh?"

"Is definitely di quickest way fi mek lots of money."

"Money isn't all, yuh know."

"What was di reason yuh seh yuh cyaan afford to go to Jamaica? I can tek care of yuh if yuh allow me."

Sheba glared at him and turned to watch the line-up at Customs. She didn't know why she had come over to him in the first place. Spider didn't notice; he was now anxiously looking for Heather.

Inside Customs, the officers searched passengers' suitcases and boxes. Heather approached a blonde, over-weight Customs officer and smiled timidly as she manoeuv-red the trolley. The woman scowled as Heather struggled to put her suitcases on the counter. Oh, God, please be kind to me, Heather prayed... Ah can't afford to be busted again... Shit Heather, stop thinking so negative, everyting gwine be all right.

"Open your suitcases," the Customs officer barked.

"All a dem?"

"Aren't you travelling with all of them?"

Of all di officers, mi haffi get a bitch. Damn it, mi hands trembling... Calm down gal, no mek she get to yuh... Oh God, if only mi hands nevah sweat so. She fumbled with the lock on the suitcase.

"What's the matter?"

"Di lock stick, officer. It seems like di suitcase nuh waan open," Heather replied sullenly.

"Really." The Customs officer's voice was cold.

Dat was a stupid ting fi say, Heather scolded herself again. If yuh continue dis way, yuh gwine arouse her suspicion... "Sorry officer, but ever so often dis stupid lock get stuck. Ah haffi get it fixed. Expensive suitcase wid cheap lock. Stupid, isn't it?"

"Really."

Yuh do it again, she cursed herself. Blabber mouth. Relax. Let di woman do her work. Jus do what Spider told yuh to do... Spider. Shit man, why do I allow yuh fi use mi like dis... Oh shut up, Heather, no one is using yuh... Yuh enjoy di challenge, yuh enjoy di money and most of all, yuh enjoy Spider.

"What's this white stuff here?"

"Wah it look like to yuh?"

"Don't get smart with me."

"Is cassava flour from cassava."

The woman glared at her but didn't say anything as she continued her search. She was at the end of her shift and she didn't have the patience to deal with this smart-ass Jamaican woman. But, as she was about to wave Heather through, her groping fingers felt something soft under the lining. A false bottom? The thought of busting this over-confident Black bitch quickly erased her tiredness. She smiled triumphantly as she pulled out several plastic bags of marijuana.

Oh God, she find dem. Heather's heart raced and her mouth went dry as she realized she faced jail again. Her dark eyes met the cold blue ones of the Customs officer. Shit.

"Rahtid." A woman standing in front of Johnny pointed at Heather being led away by two uniformed RCMP. "It look like Customs catch anodder one." The line buzzed with excitement.

God, Johnny thought to himself, please don't let dem be too hard pon her. She nevah mean no harm.

"Is people like she who come up yah and give us Black people a bad name. As long as yuh come from Ja-maica, yuh a smuggle ganja," a brown-skinned man with a bald head declared.

"Serves her right. I hope they lock her up and throw away the key. No decent girl would behave like that," a portly Black man in a suit contributed.

Heather seem to be a decent girl. Smuggling ganja is not di worst ting on earth, Johnny thought.

The sliding doors opened to reveal the Customs area.

The people in the waiting room peered in anxiously.

"Ku yah! A beef get busted!" Sandra hissed, catching sight of Heather being led away by the RCMP.

"A which gal get busted?" one of the posse asked.

"Di model gal dat did look like she have one sugar daddy supporting her."

The doors slid open again, and one of the posse shouted, "Look deh, dem a dig dung Rankin!"

Sandra and her posse hurled curses at the unhearing Customs officers. The security guards wanted to tell them to keep quiet but pretended not to notice them for fear of being similarly abused. Half an hour later, Rankin strolled outside to the boisterous shouts of the posse. He flashed them a gold-toothed smile. As he and his friends walked by, Sandra called out, "See yuh around, Sheba. Ah hope yuh don't haffi wait all night fi yuh bredda."

"He shouldn't be too long now."

"See yuh around, Spider," Sandra called to the hustler, but he didn't hear her.

Shit. Another $20,000 down di drain. Heather, yuh damn fool, yuh costing me too much money.

"Yuh fren come out yet?" Sheba asked.

"No. Wah bout yuh bredda?" he answered absently.

"See him a come deh now. What a way di bwoy get big."

Hugging Johnny, Sheba exclaimed, "Wah appen, ugly mug? Long time no see." She held him away from her and scrutinized him from head to toe. "But look how di bwoy tun big man pon me. Mi haffi look up to him face. Only yesterday mi had was to stoop dung to hear what him a seh."

Grinning shyly, Johnny mumbled, "Wah appen, big sistah? How is everyting?"

"Fine. Just fine." Turning to Spider, she said, "Johnny, meet Spider."

"Wah appen, youthman?"

"Mi all right still."

Touching Johnny's arm, Sheba turned to go. "We should be going home now. Mama's waiting on us. See yuh around, Spider."

She pushed Johnny's cart toward the door. Johnny followed closely behind her. They left the airport and went outside where several people were scrambling for taxis or waiting impatiently for buses. Johnny shivered. "Lawd God, it cold, eeh?"

Laughing, Sheba handed him a jacket. "Cold? Now is only September. Wait till it reach December and January. Not to mention February, den yuh gwine really feel cold."

"But how people manage fi live inna place like dis?" Johnny grunted between clenched teeth.

"Once yuh dress warm, it not so bad. People brave di cold months because di summer yah is nice and hot."

Shivering, her brother replied, "Mi don't tink mi can survive till summer in dis cold."

"Yuh will survive. Di winter pass off so fast dat in no time yuh will be planning fi summer."

Sheba headed for a brown van in which a Rastafarian man sat patiently behind the steering wheel.

"So a yuh man dat?"

"Bwoy, yuh fass. Him jus a good fren."

The Rastaman got out of the van and opened the back

41

of the vehicle. Taking the trolley from Sheba, he unloaded the suitcases into the van. Turning to Johnny, Sheba introduced him as Iration Dread.

"Greetings, youthman. How was yuh trip?"

"All right, I guess. But big excitement at di airport."

And with that Johnny began to tell what had happened to Heather, from the moment he had handed her the suitcases to when she was led away by the police. As the van sped along Highway 401, Johnny sat wide-eyed, watching the landscape fly past. He hardly heard Iration Dread's comments about police brutality, racial discrimination and crimes committed by gangs in the Black community. His small hometown in sunny Jamaica now seemed very far away from this bleak place. As Iration Dread turned off the highway and headed north, Johnny roused himself from his thoughts and asked, "We reach?"

"Almost dere," Sheba answered. "Just a few minutes more."

"Wow man, dis place big, eh? Seems like we a travel fi hours. So tell mi bout mama and her husband and mi new bredda and sistah."

"Don't worry bout anyting. Mama leave yuh in Jamaica when yuh was quite young, but she is still yuh madda. Karen and Joey are nice kids, yuh will get used to dem. Mr. Harry may have him faults, but him all right, and Aunt Mavis is no problem. Relax, Johnny, dis is yuh home now."

For the first time since leaving Jamaica, he relaxed. As Iration Dread's van swerved into the driveway, Johnny reached for the door handle.

The Rastaman smiled. "Hold on, youthman. Tek it

easy." Johnny settled back into his seat until the van came to a standstill. Iration Dread carried the suitcases to the door, followed by Sheba and Johnny. He bid Johnny good-night and returned to the van.

"Wait, di dread nah come inside?" Johnny asked, surprised.

"No, him haffi return to him store. Go inside, mi soon come."

"Yuh gwine give him a good-night kiss?"

"Go inside and meet the family till mi come," Sheba said as she pushed Johnny toward the door. She returned to the van, opened the door and sat beside Iration Dread. She and the Rastaman reasoned for several minutes. Looking at her watch, she said, "I have an exam early tomorrow."

The Rastaman stroked her hand gently. "Di I a leave I man already?" Although Sheba and Iration Dread had been intimate for over a year, she still got tingly just thinking about him. She had met him four years ago at a Rasta meeting and again at a party but had not really talked to him until last year at another Rasta function. When they exchanged telephone numbers she had not thought that she would get involved with him. The first time she went to his apartment they had talked for hours about Rastafari. She had felt at ease as they sat in his living room, sharing a spliff and listening to music. Eventually they had made love. Since then, Iration Dread had been part of her life. Every evening he picked her up from school or she met him at his patty store on Eglinton Avenue West. Even though she tried to convince herself that he was only a good friend and that the relationship was not permanent, she felt otherwise. Now as she sat in the van with him she wished she could go back to his apartment and make love, but she knew that wasn't possible.

"What di I tinking bout?" he asked.

"About di first time I came to di I apartment."

Pulling her closely to him, the Rastaman held her face in his hands and kissed her full on the lips. "Let's go forward to di apartment and repeat dat night," he whispered.

She felt breathless as she caressed his chest. "Ah cyaan do dat. Mi haffi go to di library tomorrow and work on a research paper."

"What time di I haffi go to di library?" he asked as he fondled her breast.

"Early in di morning."

"It won't tek long," he said as his hand slid up her skirt.

Sheba felt hot all over. She knew she had a heavy work load ahead of her the following day, but all she could think of was wanting to make love to this Rastaman. "I an I have exactly one hour," she said, looking at her watch.

"An hour it is." Iration Dread revved the engine and headed toward his apartment.

chapter *four*

The door to the Brown's home
opened and a little girl of about ten yelled, "Here he is!"
Johnny stepped into the living room. His mother stared at
him, then holding out her hands, she said, "What a way di
bwoy get big. Come give yuh madda a hug. Don't be shy.
Weh Vinette deh?"

"She outside wid she fren, di dread," Johnny answered
as his mother pressed him tightly against her hefty bosom.

"Lawd Doris, mind yuh kill di bwoy," teased her husband.

"Cho! Gwaan run up yuh mout, man. Johnny meet
your stepfaada, Harry."

"Hi, Johnny, how are you, man? Did yuh have a good
flight?"

"Fine, sah."

"Meet yuh sistah, Karen."

"Hi, Johnny. Did you bring anything for me?"

"Karen!" her mother scolded. "Joey's asleep, yuh cyan
meet him tomorrow. Yuh memba Aunt Mavis?"

Doris' younger sister came forward. Kissing Johnny on the cheek, she said, "Of course, Johnny memba me. How can he figet his favourite aunt? Right, Johnny?" She smiled at him. "So how is Jamaica?"

"Prices sky high, jobs hard fi get and nuff shooting round town. But apart from dat, Yard nice as usual."

"How is Granny and di rest of di family?" his mother asked.

"Everyone is all right. Granny send letters fi both yuh and Aunt Mavis. She — "

"Yuh see Maas D and Auntie G before yuh lef? How bout Miss May?" Mavis said, taking his arm.

"Lawd God, Mavis, Doris, give di bwoy a chance fi answer nuh man," Harry said. "As for me, Johnny, I'll see yuh tomorrow. Yuh madda and auntie obviously want yuh all to demself. Doris, don't stay out yah too long now," Harry added as he left the room.

Ignoring him, Doris continued, "Who and who come to di airport?"

"Granny and — "

"Mout-a-massy Liza never come wid her dry foot pickney dem?" Aunt Mavis cut in again. "Talking bout dry foot, wah appen to di girlfren mi hear seh yuh have in Jamaica? Mi nuh hear seh yuh box di bread out a Boysie mout."

"Mavis! Ah won't tolerate dem kind of talk. Yuh nuh see dat Johnny is jus a child."

"Yuh stay deh and tink Johnny is a lickle bwoy. Yuh nuh see him a big man now. Wait deh now, yuh nuh expect him to have a girlfren up yah?"

"Nuh bodda put nuh ideas inna him head. Him come yah fi go to school and to university. If him tink him gwine stay and form fool of himself him mek a sad mistake." Turning to Johnny she said, "Let Karen show yuh your room, yuh must be tired. And Karen, is yuh bedtime. Get up from in front of di TV and get ready fi bed. Show Johnny him room."

"So tell me wah Mama seh inna yuh letter nuh?" Mavis asked.

"Me ask yuh bout your letter?" her sister retorted.

"C'mon, Dor," Mavis pleaded. "It look like Mama arthritis get worse, not to mention her blood pressure."

"Poor Mama. At least she now have one less pickney fi worry bout. Fi yuh two bad pickney nuh mek matters better fi her."

"Lawd missis, stop pick pon me. A nuh everyone have husband like yuh fi help dem, yuh know."

"Some husband," Doris said under her breath.

"Him still arguing bout Johnny coming here to live?" Mavis whispered.

As Doris was about to answer Karen came back in the room.

"Mom, what kind of fruits are these?"

"Karen! How much time I tell yuh not to interrupt me when yuh see mi talking to someone else?"

"Sorry, Mom."

"Dem Canadian pickney nuh know nutten," Mavis offered.

"Dat is guinep. Dis one is naseberry and dat is soursop. Come taste one of di guinep — stop mek up yuh face so.

Dem Canadian nuh know nutten weh good fi dem."

Spitting the guinep into her hands, Karen wrinkled her nose. "It tastes funny, Mom."

"Funny like yuh face," Mavis teased.

"Mavis," her sister reprimanded, "don't speak to di child like dat." Softening her tone, she said, "It look like Mama still have di big guinep tree in front of di yard. Memba when we use to climb it as children?"

"Mom, you used to climb trees in Jamaica?"

"Karen, wah mi tell yuh bout interrupting when grown-ups are speaking. Didn't I send you to yuh bed?"

"But, Mom — "

"Go now, before ah give yuh a spanking."

Karen ran out of the room, crying loudly.

"Times change though, eh? Memba as children, if Mama did a talk to Miss May we couldn't put we mout inna it? One lick and we quiet fi di rest of di day. Dem pickney nowa-days nah grow wid no manners," said Mavis.

"Listen, ah gawn a bed. Mi haffi get up early and get di children ready fi church," Doris said as she got up from her chair.

"Sure, use di children as excuse. Yuh a go inside fi sweet up Harry."

"Cho. Yuh have a one track mind. Night."

Johnny had changed and come back into the living room to join his mother and aunt.

"Johnny don't stay out yah and let Mavis put any ideas inna yuh head," his mother warned. "Canada full of oppor-tunities, but yuh will haffi work hard fi achieve something."

"Oh yeah?" challenged Mavis. "Dem discriminate gainst

48

yuh in everyting. When yuh phone up bout an apartment, dem will tell yuh fi come over, but one look pon yuh and di apartment is already taken. Not to mention jobs: nuh matter how qualified yuh is, dem always waan Canadian experience. To get anyting in dis country yuh haffi work twice as hard as dem. Yuh wait till yuh start school. Dem might all waan put yuh one grade behind di odder pickney dem even though yuh probably brighter dan all di class. Listen, if any pickney call yuh nigger, just chop him inna him head."

"Mavis! Stop tell di child foolishness. Canada is not like Jamaica where yuh have all kind a hooligans. Mi rather deh amongst white people dan some of dese riff-raff dat a come up from Jamaica. As far as me concern, dem shouldn't allow dem fi come to a nice country like dis. Jus trust God, yuh hear and everyting will be all right."

"God? Yuh tink God can — "

"Mavis, das enuff. Good night, Johnny. Sleep good."

"Yuh nah tell mi good night too?" called Mavis.

"No rest fi di heathen," her sister retorted. Just then the door opened and Sheba entered the room. "Speaking of heathen, look who cometh. Weh yuh a do pon road dis time a di night? Yuh won't leave out of dem Rasta company?"

Sheba ignored her mother.

"Wah appen Sheba, how's Iration Dread?" Mavis asked.

Mavis' question hit an old sore point with Doris. "Look wah mi come to! Mi decent pickney come put herself inna dis Rasta stupidness. For somebody who have so much ambition I don't see how yuh can mix up wid dem kind of people. Rasta nuh put yuh nowhere in dis society. Dem nuh have no ambition. Everybody look down pon dem."

"Mama, please don't start on dat tonight."

"Sheba, don't pay her no mind," Mavis consoled.

"Sheba?" Doris sucked her teeth. "Me christen dis girl Vinette Caroline Smith, and all of a sudden she become Sheba Tafari. Yuh tink anybody want Rasta fi look after dem pickney inna daycare?"

"Mama, yuh should get used to me being a Rasta. Nuh matter what yuh seh, ah is a Rasta and ah gwine mek it as a Rasta. Nutten gwine change mi mind. Mi is proud to be a Rasta and determined fi graduate from college and own my own daycare centre."

"Don't get mi wrong. Mi proud a yuh and mi love yuh very much, but mi wish yuh nevah haffi mix up wid all dem Rasta," her mother said in a tired voice.

"Johnny, mi nah see yuh till tomorrow night, so tek care," Sheba said as she turned to leave the living room.

"But tomorrow's Sunday. Don't tell mi dat dem go to school up yah pon Sunday."

Sheba laughed. "No, but mi haffi go to di library as soon as it open. Mi working on a research paper."

"My sistah owning a daycare! Wait till ah write and tell Sweetie and Boysie."

"Ah don't even graduate yet much less fi own a daycare. Mi have a long way fi go before dat can happen."

Aunt Mavis smiled proudly at her niece. "You'll mek it one of dese days."

"Not if she continue wid dis Rasta foolishness."

"Here we go again," Sheba said. "Night, everybody," she added as she went downstairs.

"Miself haffi turn in too. Night, Johnny, Mavis."

"Just me and you leave now, Johnny. So tell Aunt Mavis wah Boysie and Sweetie up to dese days? Yuh mean di no good pickney dem couldn't drop me a line?"

Sheba sat behind her desk, staring at the textbooks in front of her. She was having a hard time concentrating. Her thoughts kept going back to the passionate lovemaking she had shared with Iration Dread a few hours ago. Roots wine... ital pizza... one of the best draws of herb she had ever smoked. Her mind and her body had belonged to him. She had lain on the carpet as he slowly undressed her in the candlelight. Picking her up, he had carried her to his bedroom where he gently placed her on the bed. She had clasped her hands around his neck and pulled him down on top of her. As she had undressed him his hands caressed her breasts and thighs. "Oh God," she had sighed softly as he penetrated her.

But as she lay in the bed beside him, both of them soaked with sweat, the telephone rang. He rolled over and picked up the receiver. From the tone when he answered she knew he had not expected the call. He put the receiver down slowly. After a few seconds he said, "Dat was Valrie. She is at di bus station. I have to go pick her up."

The reference to his wife jolted Sheba. She fumbled with her clothes as he told her he hadn't known that his wife was coming to Toronto from Detroit. They sat in silence as he drove Sheba home. The van pulled up into the driveway, and Sheba flung the door open and hurried out. She didn't hear him promise to call her the following day.

She fumbled with the key in the lock but composed herself for a few seconds before she faced her family. She didn't look back as the van drove off.

Now she sat in her bedroom, away from her family and Iration Dread, the tears flowing down her face. Although she had known that Iration Dread had a wife and seven children living in Detroit, all she had let herself see was a single man living alone in a place where she felt warm and comfortable. The only times she had to face that he was married were the rare times his wife came to Toronto. Usually, when his wife came to the city, Iration Dread would let Sheba know in advance. This was the first time she had not called him before she came over. From the telephone conversation Sheba could tell that Iration Dread was angry about the unexpected visit.

But as much as Sheba had come to feel a need for Iration Dread, she knew that his wife had a right to be angry too. After all, wasn't Sheba the other woman? Damn, how she hated those words. But she had known all along that Iration Dread had a wife and family, and tonight all her pretence that he was just a friend, a temporary need, mocked her from deep inside her pain.

Why do we women, you and me, sistah, allow ourself to be hurt dis way? Even as she asked the question, Sheba knew that she couldn't do without Iration Dread. Not yet.

chapter five

Johnny lay in bed listening to his
mother singing gospel songs as she fixed breakfast in the
kitchen. Joey was asleep in the other bed. Getting up,
Johnny stood by the window and watched his step-father
raking fallen leaves. The wind blew gently, scattering leaves
across the lawn. His stepfather cursed loudly as he tried to
control them with his rake.

"Good morning, Johnny," said Doris, entering the
room. "Yuh sleep good last night?"

"Yes, Mama." Johnny's voice was soft.

"So how yuh like yuh new home so far?" Without
waiting for an answer, she continued, "Yuh goin to love
living in Toronto. Wait till yuh go to school tomorrow and
start meeting new frens. Get ready fi church and den come
eat yuh breakfast." Walking over to Joey's bed, she shook
him until he woke. "Joey, baby, get up and get dressed fi
church." On her way out, she added, "Unnu nuh bodda stay
in yah till di breakfast get cold."

Joey sat up in bed and rubbed his eyes. Noticing Johnny for the first time he stared at him. "Who're you?" he said.

"Mi name Johnny," Johnny stammered, a bit stunned at his brother's forwardness. "How old are you?"

"I'm six and a half. I'm going to be seven in December. Mom told us about you. Dad says there're too many of Mom's family living here already. He says, first there was Vinette, then Aunt Mavis and now you."

Johnny had gotten up in the night to use the bathroom and had heard his mother and her husband shouting at each other. "Mi nevah like di idea of him coming fi live yah," Harry had said. "Him is mi son and him have every right to live wid di rest of di family," his mother had shot back.

"Why doesn't my Daddy like you guys living here?" Joey asked.

Aunt Mavis stuck her head through the open door and said, "Hurry up, you guys. Yuh madda having a fit downstairs. Di breakfast is getting cold."

"Good morning, Aunt Mavis." Joey kissed her on the cheek. As Joey left the room, Mavis turned to Johnny and said, "Mi hear wah Joey say to you lickle while. Don't be upset, him jus a kid. Him nuh mean anyting by it."

"And what about Missa Harry? Him is not a kid."

"Well, you have fi understand Harry and where him is coming from. Mi guess him figure dat when him marry Doris him nevah expect fi marry her sister, son and daughter. Is a big responsibility to tek care of so many people. Grant you, mi is only here on di weekends because mi have a live-in job. Sheba go to school full-time. It hard fi her fi work and go to school at di same time. Any money she mek during di summer jus go fi her studies. She still have a few more years fi go. And dere is you."

"But how you and Sheba put up wid it?"

"What choice mi have? Ah cyaan rent a room fi just di weekends. Mi trying fi save money fi send fi Sweetie and Boysie. Besides, mi nuh too straight yah, and so mi cyaan get nutten but domestic work and di pay is pretty low. Poor Sheba have it so hard. She want fi graduate from school so bad dat she working two jobs during di summer jus fi pay off her studies. No way she cyan pay di rent plus school fees. And being a Rasta doesn't help her situation round yah."

"How Mama feel bout all dis?"

"Yuh nuh know yuh madda like I do. She would nevah put aside her family fi Harry. She figure seh she work jus as hard as him fi buy dis house, so she have di right fi have her family wid her. She is a strong and determined woman. Mi know it's hard fi her fi see her family torn apart like dis, but ah guess she figure seh one day tings will work out."

"Mi wish mi did know all dis before mi come up yah. Granny nevah tell mi nutten like dis."

"Mama don't know nutten about dis and it is to stay dat way, yuh hear me? As far as she concern we're all contented here. Anyway, what seh we go get some breakfast? Give Auntie a big hug and nuh worry bout nutten. Everyting gwine be all right."

After Doris and her family left for church, Mavis sat in the kitchen sipping a cup of coffee. She put her mind to her conversation with Johnny. Since she had been living in

Toronto, some five years now, she had been trying to straighten out her life. She had known that it was going to be difficult, but she hadn't expected it would take so long. For the first time, however, it seemed that she was finally going to achieve her dreams. Months ago, when she heard about the Canadian government's amnesty program for illegal immigrants, she had immediately applied for amnesty through an immigration consultant. She prayed day and night for a letter to come from the government, informing her that she had been granted landed status.

Mavis sighed as she got up to wash the cup she had been using. She yearned to see her children again. As she looked around the house, she hoped that one day she too would have the security of a good home, with a husband and children. She did not envy Doris, but she too had worked very hard to achieve similar status. Mavis sighed again.

The next morning, Johnny admired his new clothes in the mirror. Dark brown pants, beige shirt and matching socks. The tight shoes he had worn up from Jamaica were replaced with ones that were comfortable but stylish. As he combed his hair, he smiled and thought, if only Boysie and di odders could see mi now.

Today was the first day of school and he was scared. As he walked the short distance to school, his heart thumped. Only three days ago he and Boysie and the others had been sitting in the Carib Theatre, enjoying one of their favourite movies, "The Good, the Bad and the Ugly." Now he was in a different city, in a different country, surrounded by a different kind of people.

He felt a lump in his throat as he opened the door to the English class. The teacher and students stared at him as he entered the room. Looking around the sea of white faces, Johnny spotted a seat in a corner. As he slunk toward the chair, he felt himself sweat. The teacher gave what was meant to be a reassuring smile and said, "It looks like we've got a new student, class. What's your name?"

"Johnny Smith, sah." Johnny replied huskily.

Hearing his unfamiliar accent, the students looked at him curiously. Johnny slumped in his chair, hoping to avoid his teacher's eyes.

"I'm Mr. McClear. Johnny, are you familiar with the works of Shakespeare? I realize that in the Islands — " He stared at Johnny without blinking. "You're from the Islands, aren't you?" His tone indicated that he was stating a fact not asking a question. He waited for confirmation.

Stuttering nervously, Johnny replied, "Yes, sah. I'm from Jamaica. I have read *Julius Caesar, Comedy of Errors*, and *Hamlet.* In Jamaica we — "

The rest was lost in the sound of the bell and the rush of students toward the door. The teacher's voice rose faintly above the noise, reminding them of tomorrow's assignment. "Here," he said, handing Johnny a photocopied page. "Take this. It's due tomorrow." Picking up his books and papers he left a puzzled Johnny scanning a list of questions. Johnny left the classroom, half-stumbling his way down the corridor as other students brushed past him, hurrying to reach the next class on time.

Several months later Johnny sat in the school yard watching other students play baseball. If he had been back home in Jamaica he would have tried to make a pass at the Black girl going by, but today he pretended not to notice her. She stopped in front of him.

"Hi, my name's Marsha. What's yours?"

"Johnny."

"Can I sit down, Johnny?" Marsha asked, smiling down at him.

"Sure. Why not," Johnny replied, surprised.

"Something the matter?"

"No."

"You seem so far away. Are you sure you're all right?

"Just tinking bout Jamaica and di nice time mi use to have dere."

"You can have a nice time here too. Wait till you start making friends and going places. You're just having culture shock. Happens to all of us when we first come. Ten years ago, I felt exactly like you, but now I like Toronto a lot."

"Ah meet frens, but is not di same. Is not just di difference in di country or di people. Is more dan dat. Yuh see, mi grow wid Granny and mi cousins in Jamaica. Granny was everyting to me."

"You really love her, don't you?"

"Very much. Is di first time in twelve years mi see mi madda. Living wid her and her husband is not di same as living wid Granny and di others. Mi know Mama is trying her best to mek me feel at home, but mi is not use to her. Mi try to be frenly to Karen and Joey but dem just ignore me. Missa Harry don't even like me," Johnny sighed.

"Come on, Johnny, don't say that. Besides, it can't be that bad."

"Him give me a whole heap of work while Joey and Karen watch TV all day. If yuh only know. Di only person mi can talk to is mi big sistah, Sheba. She's studying daycare at Ryerson. She use to live wid us, but now dat she have her own apartment ah hardly see her. Aunt Mavis seems to understand what mi goin through. Mi like talking to her. She really nice, but she has two jobs, so she hardly ever home."

"So how's school?"

"Ah can't mek head nor tail of di school work. It seems so different from di work in Jamaica. And every time ah open mi mout di white kids stare at me. Sometimes ah know di answer to a question but mi fraid fi open mi mout."

"I know what you mean. You've got to ask the teacher to explain the stuff to you after class. What I don't like is when the white kids tease us and call us names."

"Dem really do dat?"

"Oh yeah. Now it's not so bad, but when I first came here it was awful. They called us names like "nigger" and "chocolate face." There were lots of fights. Sometimes we had to run home just to keep from getting into a fight. If a Black and a white kid fought, the Black kid would get sent to the principal, but the white kids — nothing would happen to them."

"And di homework — because mi don't understand di work it seem impossible. If Sheba was around more often mi sure she could help me."

"Tell you what, maybe I'm not as smart as your sister, but I bet I can help you. Come over to my place on Saturday, and we can do our homework together, and maybe later on, if it isn't too late, we can go to the Roller Palace with the other kids. Can you skate?"

"No, but ah cyan learn. You mean yuh madda allow yuh fi bring over bwoyfrens?"

"You aren't my boyfriend, you're in my class. Here in Toronto parents aren't as strict as in Jamaica. My parents let me have dates as long as I get home on time."

"Does dat mean we have a date?" Johnny put his arm casually around her shoulders.

"You can call it that."

"Does dat mean we now bwoyfren and girlfren?"

Marsha slowly shook his arm away. "Of course not. I'm going with somebody."

"Mi cyan show you a really nice time. Yuh boyfren soft to runnings, man. Nevah fear, Johnny Lover is here!"

"You've got a sweet mouth. Here's my phone number. Call before you come, okay?"

"Yes, princess. Ah looking forward to it."

Marsha smiled shyly. "See you Saturday."

Sheba lay on the sofa in the living room of the basement apartment she shared with Iration Dread. She had just come home from school and was too tired to change her clothes. She felt hungry. She had telephoned the ital store to ask Iration Dread to bring home supper, but Mikey, his assistant, told her Iration had left several hours ago and he didn't know where he had gone. Strange, Sheba thought, it wasn't like him to leave without letting anyone at the store know where he was going.

Since they had been living together, almost ten months now, their relationship had grown stronger. They encouraged each other in their work, but it seemed like her life revolved around his. There were times when she missed not having her family with her, but her mother didn't approve of her living with him. Sometimes Sheba wondered if she had made the right decision. She fell asleep, thinking about the changes in her life.

The telephone rang. Sheba groggily answered. It took her a few seconds to recognise the older Rastafarian woman's voice.

"Wah appening?" It was Sister B from the Ethiopian Orthodox Church. She really liked this woman.

"Wake up, man. Yuh sleep too much."

"What time is it?"

"Almost twelve o'clock."

"Ah wonder if Iration Dread come back to the store yet?"

"What time di store lock up?"

"Usually bout ten o'clock, but sometimes if dem have customers dem would stay a bit longer."

Sister B laughed. "It look like yuh man a sleep out tonight wid anodder woman."

"No man, him not like dat. Him probably still deh at di store. Mi did call him earlier, but him wasn't dere. Him probably soon come home. Anyway, how yuh doing? How come yuh nevah come a service last Sunday?"

"Me and di man have one big fight di night before. Him nuh give me a black eye and buss up mi mout."

"God, Sister B, yuh gwine mek di man kill yuh? Why don't yuh leave him?"

"And go where wid five pickney? Mi cyaan leave mi house wid all mi furniture and go pon di road wid mi pickney dem."

"Yuh can't get him fi leave di house?"

"Yuh know how much time mi pack up him tings and run him out of di house? Him used to leave and go stay wid him brethren dem, but nowadays instead of leaving, him jus beat me up."

"Yuh alright now?"

"Di mout a heal up and di swelling a go dung."

"Dem man yah wicked. How him cyan go a church every Sunday and worship God and still a beat up woman?"

"Di amount of time dis man beat me up mi stop count. One time him kick me so hard him bruk him toe."

"Him should a bruk him foot. If any man ever lick me, mi goin haffi kill him."

"Ah used to say dat before mi start have children. Yuh lucky yuh man nuh beat yuh. Iration Dread a decent Rastaman."

"Since we a deal, bout two years now, we have nuff arguments, but him nevah put him hands pon me."

"When yuh gwine give him a youth? About time, yuh know."

"Now yuh sound like him. Right now di only ting pon my mind is to graduate from school and open a daycare. Mi cyaan tink bout youth right now."

"How him feel bout dat?"

"Him want me fi finish school, but deep down mi know seh him would a want mi fi have a youth wid him. Mi tell him seh him have seven pickney, him nuh need nuh more. Right now, mi can't have no youth wid nuh married man."

"Den why deal wid him?"

Sheba paused for a few seconds. "Ah guess mi figure dat one day mi will find a single Rastaman like Iration Dread who mi cyan start mi family wid."

"Right now yuh need a nice relationship wid a man dat yuh check for, even if it's only temporary."

Sheba paused again. "Maybe yuh right. Nuff times mi question why mi even deal wid him knowing dat him have a wife. Mi would a nevah deal wid him if him was living wid him family in di city."

"How often she come to Toronto?"

"Not dat often."

"Him deal wid her when she's here?"

"When him use to have him own apartment dat was where she would stay. Since we a live together she nuh come over."

"How yuh know dat?"

"Come to tink bout it, I don't. Him sleep yah every night except — "

"Except tonight, right? Maybe she is in town and him is wid her now."

"Without even telling me dat him not coming home? Ah find dat hard fi believe. Where would he go wid her? Definitely not a hotel."

"Maybe one of him brethren house."

"Di only brethren him really move wid is a dread name Ibo out in di west end. Ah find it hard fi believe dat him would a stay out all night and nuh even call, knowing dat mi would a worry."

"Dat's not unusual. Him only being like a typical man. Him figure seh him is a big man, him nuh haffi give yuh no explanation."

Glancing at the clock on the wall, Sheba clenched the phone. "Two o'clock already. Him nevah stay out dis late before. Ah wonder if Beast pick him up pon di road?"

"If police did raid di store yuh would a hear someting. Nutten nuh happen to him, man. Him wife in di city and him deh wid her. Listen, mi will talk to yuh tomorrow, it a get late."

"Yuh a come to church next Sunday?"

"Maybe, depends on how mi feel."

"Ah understand. Ah will give yuh a call tomorrow when mi come home from school."

"Don't stay up all night and worry bout dis man. Him not worth it. Eventually him will call yuh. Go to yuh bed and get a good night sleep."

"I hear yuh. Night, Sister B."

Sheba sat staring past the television, Sister B's words echoing in her thoughts. "No, he wouldn't do dis to me," she said out loud. "But where di hell is he?" She got up and paced the living room. She felt hungry but was too worried to eat. Although she knew it was pointless calling the store, she had to do something. She dialled the number and got Mikey's voice on the answering machine. "Dread out," he said, after announcing the store hours. She smiled. Mikey was a humble, irie, *single* Rastaman. Why couldn't she have fallen in love with someone like him?

"Iration Dread, I hate you," she yelled at the wall, forgetting that her cousin, Kingsley, and his girlfriend lived

64

with their son upstairs in the three-bedroom flat.

Three o'clock. Iration where are you? She went into the kitchen and made a tofu sandwich. She bit into the sandwich, then put it back on the plate. What she needed was a spliff. Rummaging through the drawer where Iration Dread kept the herbs, she picked up a long bud. Picking up the cutting board and the knife, she sat at the kitchen table again. After the herb was finely cut, she rolled a long spliff in a corn leaf. She took a pull, inhaled deeply and felt it course through her body. Before meeting Iration Dread she hadn't been a big smoker, but now she smoked at least two spliffs a day.

Why did I get involved with yuh, Iration Dread? Because yuh need a nice relationship. Many times she had told him how uncomfortable she felt about having a relationship with a married man. He would counter, "Seven woman fi one man, according to di Scriptures." He had often told her that she was his wife and getting as much love as Valrie and their seven children. How is it, she wondered, dat is always men dat interpret di Scriptures?

She got up and looked at the clock again. Five-thirty. At this point she gave up on the idea that Iration Dread was in hospital or in jail. Now she was convinced he must be at Ibo's house. Was Valrie with him? Why hadn't he called her? She had to find out. She picked up the telephone, began to dial. She put the phone down. No, it was too early in the morning to call, she thought. She would wait until six o'clock. She had waited all night, another half an hour would not make any difference.

Twice, after terrible arguments, Iration Dread had

packed his things and said he was moving out. She remembered crying all night. Now she wished he had moved out. One minute to six. As she dialled Ibo's number, her heart pounded. She apologized to Sharon, Ibo's girlfriend, for calling so early in the morning, then asked to speak to Iration Dread.

Sheba tensed as she heard his voice on the telephone. From his tone she knew that Valrie was lying beside him in bed. Trying to control her voice, she told him to come and pick up his things. As she hung up the telephone the tears streamed down her face. Wiping her eyes, she got up, went to the closet, pulled out Iration's clothes and packed them in his suitcase. Then she went into the kitchen, took down his appliances and utensils and packed them in a box. Placing his suitcase and the box in the living room, she sighed.

chapter six

Iration Dread sat behind the counter. This morning was like every other morning. He and Mikey had baked patties, puddings and cocoa bread. Instead of making the usual beetroot and carrot juice for lunch, Iration had made granola and soursop juice. Normally, he made these juices on the weekends or for afternoons when he had a much larger crowd. In the afternoon, he cooked ital stew or rice and peas with mixed vegetables for the lunch crowd — the young men who were just getting to know ital food. It gave Iration Dread great pleasure to see them savouring it for the first time. It reminded him of his own childhood in Jamaica.

Every day after school he and his friends had visited the Rasta camp before going home. He had been struck by the dignity and pride Rastafarians carried themselves with and felt at home in their humble zinc-roofed houses. He would never forget the nights he had spent in bed, listening to the powerful, rhythmic Nyah Binghi drums, chants accentuating every beat, the congregation recounting their glorious African heritage and culture, telling of the magnificent ancestral home in Zion. He had pictured himself among the congregation, dressed in red, gold and green, chanting and dancing around the tabernacle while the fire burned outside.

On his first day at the Rasta camp Iration Dread had vowed he would become a Rastaman. Although he had stopped eating meat and cutting his hair at the age of sixteen, he hadn't started locksing his hair for another two years, a year before he came to Toronto to join his family. As one of a small group of young Rastafarians in Toronto at the time he had faced many challenges. His inspiration had been his memories of the Rasta camp.

As two young customers entered the shop Iration Dread smiled. He felt that it was his duty to carry on the legacy of the Rasta camp, and he felt honoured to have found ways to do it.

"Wah appen, Iration Dread? Wah di man a seh?" Chuckie was a regular.

"One love, youthman."

"Hail, Iration Dread. Wah on di menu today?" Bigger asked.

"Rasta love, youthman. Food is di staff of life, as long as di man eat fi live and nuh live fi eat."

"In dat case, it seem like Bigger live fi eat. Look at di bwoy stomach, eh?"

"Di man is jus fit, not fat, right Bigger?"

"Seen, Iration Dread." Bigger glared at Chuckie, daring him to say otherwise.

Within a few minutes Tafari Ital shop filled with young

men waiting to order lunch and chatting idly with friends. The shop was the place to catch up on news and to listen to heavy reggae music from the juke box in the corner. It was the only place in Toronto where they could get ital food and Iration Dread was like a brother to them.

Johnny walked along Eglinton Avenue West where the West Indian stores were located. Instead of him going on a school trip that day, his mother had sent him to the tailor shop on Marlee. Glancing in shop windows, he marvelled at the variety of clothes for sale. Other windows, filled with pastries and other tropical foods, reminded him of Jamaica. This was the first time he had seen so many Black people in one area in Toronto. Eglinton seemed so different from Scarborough where he lived.

Inside Tafari Ital shop, Chuckie and Bigger were sampling the shop's ital patties. Licking his fingers, Chuckie said, "Iration Dread, di man is di best ital chef inna all of Toronto. No, mek dat Canada. Dem ital patties yah well irie."

"Seen youthman. Ital is vital," the Rastaman said in acknowledgement.

"Yeah, man, dem pattie yah well irie. Wah di man put in dem?" Bigger asked, picking up his third patty.

"Dat is a trade secret. Everything good fi di structure inna it," Iration Dread said, smiling smugly.

"Come on, Iration Dread, tell us di ingredients. We nah tell anyone di secret," Chuckie promised.

"Is nuh so much di ingredients but di ability fi blend dem up right."

"One ting mi know fi sure is dat it have no salt in it," Bigger said.

"No salt, and it taste so good? A true, Iration?"

"Seen youthman. I and I nuh eat salt. Most food have salt already. Derefore yuh nuh need fi add salt. Babylon condition di people fi add salt in everyting dem eat. Das why dem have so much high blood pressure. A lot of di meat dem a feed people have chemicals. Yuh nuh see how dem always a go a doctor fi all sort of chemicals. It's a business: feed di people junk so as fi keep di doctor in business."

"Di man right, dread," Bigger replied.

"A true, man. Big business fi di establishment," Chuckie said. Peering through the window, he beckoned the others. "No Johnny from Jones Town dat?" Pushing his head through the open door, he yelled, "Johnny, Johnny, come yah, man!"

Johnny spun around and was surprised to see Chuckie, the crown-and-anchor dealer from Benbow Street. He hugged him in disbelief.

"Wah appen, Chuckie? Di man disappear from Yard jus like dat." Johnny clicked his fingers.

"Yeah, man, Jamdown did a get too hot fi me. After di big shootout mi did haffi shake di area. So tell me, when di man forward a Toronto?"

"Bout a year now. Mi live wid mi modder and her family in Scarborough, pon Huntington Avenue."

"So how was Yard when yuh was leaving it? Any word pon Sala?"

"Yeah, Boysie write and tell mi dat dem find Sala guilty of robbery and assault."

"Sala? Miss May's son dat live pon Benbow Street?"

"Rahtid. Bigger, mi figet yuh come from Jones Town too. Yuh nuh memba Johnny?" Chuckie asked.

"Nuh really. Which street yuh come from a Jones Town?"

"Benbow Street."

"Me know a Yard pon Benbow Street wid a big mango tree dat we use fi raid."

"Dat a mi Granny yard."

"Dat is yuh Granny? She still a cook dem nice dumpling and saltfish?" Bigger rubbed his stomach.

"Di man love food, eh?"

"How yuh tink mi get so big?"

"A one ting wid Granny, she will allow di youth dem fi raid di mango tree but when yuh play a trick pon someone or skip school, she will drape yuh up real hard," Chuckie said.

Looking at his watch, Johnny said, "Listen, man, mi haffi mek a move now. Mi madda send me to — "

"Yuh can't leave yet till yuh eat one of Iration Dread ital patty. Di best ital chef in di whole of Canada."

Chuckie turned toward the counter. "Iration, give mi brethren a patty and one of di man famous fruit juice."

"Wah appen, Johnny? How is yuh sistah?"

"Wah appen, Iration Dread? Ah guess Sheba all right, yuh know. So, di man don't come round nuh more, eh?"

"Just movements." Iration Dread didn't want to talk about his personal life.

"So wah kind of juice di man want? Dere is mango, papaya, sour sop, beet root and carrot. Dis week's special is granola."

"Let mi try di granola. Mi nevah drink dat before."
Taking a glass from the Rastaman, Johnny downed the
drink. "Dis juice nice, eh. Wah di ingredients?"

Chuckie and Bigger looked at each other then yelled
out, "Trade secret." Everyone in the shop laughed while
Bigger explained the joke to Johnny.

"How much mi owe di man?" said Chuckie.

"Five bucks, youthman."

Chuckie pulled out his wallet and handed Iration a
fifty-dollar bill from a stack of fifties and hundreds. "Rahtid,"
said Johnny, "Chuckie, yuh wallet fat, eh?"

"Yeah, man. Mi deh pon some big runnings."

"Wah kind of runnings?"

"Some big business. Yuh know me is a hustler from
morning: anyting a gwaan, mi haffi inna it. Johnny, di man
have a number? Here, write it in mi lickle black book. A nuff
contact mi have in dis yah book, yuh know," he bragged.

"Stick close to me Johnny, and it gwine be jus like old
times," Chuckie added, opening the glass door. The three
walked out together.

The younger crowd soon gave way to an older one of
Rastafarians and non-Rastafarians coming from work. They
ate as they discussed local and international news. Some
stayed until late at night, while others left and still others
took their places. The shop reminded them of what they
had left behind in Jamaica, and although most had shared
tables the day before, they greeted each other as if they
hadn't seen each other in a long time. They ordered, settling
comfortably in their seats, and waited for Wolde or Big
Dread to bring up the day's topic. Today it was Wolde's
turn.

Wolde worked hard to convince his brethren and sistren to accept the teachings of the Ethiopian Orthodox Church. Established in the early seventies in Toronto, its ancient Christian practices dated back to the fourth century. Like earlier Ethiopian emperors, Emperor Haile Selassie I was the Patriarch in the church. The merits of Rastafari versus Christianity had heated many discussions in Jamaica and in the shop. While the debaters agreed that Christianity was used to subjugate Black people, the question of Rastas' involvement in the church had divided the debaters into two groups. The pro-church group, usually led by Wolde, would argue that Jah Haile Selassie I had set an example by baptizing in the church and that therefore Rastafarians should baptize in the church, to enter Zion.

The anti-church group, usually led by Big Dread, claimed that the Pope — thought of as the Devil — was the head of all churches. If Rastafarians became involved in the church they would be bowing to the devil. No, the Order of Nyah Binghi, following an ancient African tradition, was the only true church for Rastafarians.

Looking around the crowded shop, Wolde cleared his throat. Some patrons kept eating; others listened to the juke box or had absorbed themselves in conversation. Raising his voice above the din, Wolde said, "What a way Metro's finest getting outta hand."

"Wah di matter, Wolde?" Tuffy from the table across the room called out. Everyone's attention had turned to Wolde. He cleared his throat again.

"Mi hear on di news a few nights ago seh dat a cop shoot a Black youth in a club downtown."

"Which youth dat?" Big Dread asked.

"A Black youth from out East." Wolde continued.

"According to di news, di youth hit one of di cops wid a billy club, and di cop fired fi defend himself."

"Bullshit. Nutten more dan dem was beating up di poor youth and di youth use di billy club fi defend himself. Yuh mean so much of dem couldn't handle one youth dat dem haffi shoot him down in cold blood?" Tuffy demanded.

"Dese cops nuh care. As far as dem concern him is jus anodder trouble-making nigger. Dem nuh even charge di Beasts dem. Instead, dem a go have a inquest, but we all know seh nutten nah go come out of dat. Dem will nevah charge no cop fi a Black man," Wolde went on.

"Is about time Black people stand up fi dem rights. Memba in '73 when dem raid Winston gates and lock up me and bout nine other man?" Iration Dread said, sitting down at Wolde's table.

"Fi wha?" Tuffy asked.

"According to dem, dem did a look fi guns."

"Dem find anyting?" Wolde asked.

"Find wah? All dem find was a ounce of herbs and a few spliffs."

"And dem lock up ten man fi dat? Dem nuh have nutten better fi do?" Big Dread said.

"Memba di three Black youth dem seh shoot di cab driver? Well, during dat time di cops raid nuff gates and nuff man get charge fi herbs."

"Me memba dat time quite well. During dat time no taxi driver nuh want fi tek up any Black man in him cab. Taxi drivers from all over Toronto stage a big demonstration downtown. Less dan a year afterward a white man shoot dung a sixteen-year-old Jamaican youth inna cold blood," Wolde added.

"Me memba di incident. Wah appen to dat case?" Big Dread asked.

"Wah yuh expect? Nutten of course. Dem seh di white man was crazy. Ah di first time mi see so much Black people so angry. Dem stage a big demonstration at City Hall," said Tuffy.

"Right now, demonstration is foolishness. Look how long Black people a protest and no change nuh come bout. Look wah appen to Martin Luther King? Is time Black people stand up fi dem rights." Iration Dread got up from the table.

"Das exacly wah Bob Marley did a tell dem at di concert at Convocation Hall. Remember wah appen three days after di show?" Wolde leaned forward to make his point.

Iration Dread paused on his way back to the grill. "Yeah, di papers and TV, led by di *Globe and Mail,* launch a vicious, racist attack gainst Rastas, saying how I and I a criminal and dat I and I a Metro's number one problem. After dat, Rastas go through nuff harassment. About time I and I stand up fi I and I rights."

"Wah di I suggest?"

Before Wolde could answer, Sheba and Akilah entered the shop. A faint smile creased Iration Dread's face as he saw the Rastawomen come in. Sheba smiled shyly at him as she and Akilah greeted the men.

"Wah Tuffy arguing bout now?" Akilah asked as she went to sit beside him.

"I man not arguing, Sistah Akilah. I man believe in

talking up fi mi rights. Is bout time Black people defend demself and stop dis demonstration foolishness. It nevah help Black people in di United States in di '60s and it nah go help us inna di '70s."

"Yuh hear bout di demonstration dem a plan fi di Black youth dem kill?" Sheba asked.

"Who a plan it?" Wolde wanted to know.

"A group of Black people calling a meeting fi discuss di shooting."

"Wah deh fi discuss? All dem haffi do is mek an example of di cop dat murder di youth and bag him, New York style," Tuffy said.

"Nutten much nah go come from di inquest, but mi nuh agree wid bagging, as yuh call it," Akilah said.

"Yuh tink Black people should siddung and mek di Beast gun dem down everyday, eh?" Tuffy raised his voice. "Every time a Black man commit a crime it mek front page news, but when injustice is done to a Black man, dem waan cover it up. Memba in '72 how dem handle di lickle Black hockey player name Paul Smither?"

The men nodded.

"Yeah, man, I man memba," said Wolde. "Dem charge di youth fi murder following a racial fight in which di white youth was killed. Afterwards dem reduce di charge to manslaughter 'cause di hospital people seh dat di youth dead when him choke on him own vomit. Even though di fight was provoked by racism di Black youth was convicted."

"Dat go to show dat Black people will never get any justice inna Canadian court. Look wah appen to di dread dem charge fi di shooting at di Mississauga party last year?"

"Wah appen to dat case?" Sheba asked.

"Yuh know dem party shooting deh. Innocent man sent to prison while di real killer roam di street. All it tek is fi di police fi coerce a so-called eyewitness fi testify gainst any man dem decide is guilty." Wolde paused to take a sip of juice.

"Dat may be so, but mi tink is bout time di youths dem behave demself and stop kill off dem brothers and sisters. Why dem haffi carry guns to parties, anyway?"

"A man haffi defend himself, Sistah Sheba. Wah if someone out to get yuh and yuh go to di party unprotected?" said Big Dread.

"Dat is di problem, Big Dread. Every gunman a go a party wid guns fi defend himself while innocent people a go fi enjoy demself. Usually a innocent people get killed at dese dances," Akilah retorted. "Any gunman who lurk inna dark and shoot people is a coward. Dis is di same man who fraid fi defend himself gainst police when dem a beat dem up."

"I man agree wid yuh, dawta, but I man still tink dat a man haffi defend himself when him go a session," Big Dread said. "Wah if — "

"Wah if nutten. All unnu gunman are di same," Akilah put in.

Glaring at her, Big Dread shouted, "Mind wah yuh seh, dawta!"

Iration Dread, now sitting quietly behind the counter, shifted the conversation to the demonstration being staged downtown. Tuffy and the others picked up the cue.

Mavis and Doris sat quietly, absorbed in the television.

"Good evening, Mama, Aunt Mavis," Johnny greeted them as he entered the house.

"Evening, Johnny," Mavis answered.

"So how did yuh visit to di tailor shop pon Eglinton go?" his mother asked.

"Okay," Johnny shrugged.

"Just okay?"

"By di time mi reach, di tailor shop was closed."

"From morning yuh leave di house, where did yuh go, eh?"

"Ah was passing dis ital shop on Eglinton and mi meet two friends from Jamaica and — "

"Imagine mi send out dis bwoy fi go tek him measurement and instead him spend di whole day a Rasta shop. Yuh tink mi tek yuh from Jamaica fi yuh come a Toronto and keep Rasta company? Mi hear how dat Missa Butty send yuh a Rasta camp, but yuh wait till mi go a Jamaica. Him gwine get a piece of mi mind. Nuh bodder mix up wid dem bwoys deh pon Eglinton. All dem do is smoke ganja all day and chat foolishness."

"Mama, dat nuh true. Iration Dread reason a lot bout di Bible. Him seh dat Black people is di chosen people and dat Rastafari di true and living God."

"Yuh a call me a liar, eh? Mi nuh waan nuh Rasta talk inna mi house. Before dat mi send yuh back a Jamaica."

Turning to her sister, she continued, "Can yuh imagine, dis bwoy a call me a liar and pon top of dat, a blaspheme, eeh?"

"All right, Doris. Cool down, man. Johnny nevah mean

fi call yuh a liar. All he is saying is dat — "

"Now yuh a pick up fi di bwoy? Yuh soon start pick up fi di Rasta bwoy dem too. Who knows, maybe yuh a smoke ganja yuhself."

"Doris, dat nuh true and yuh know it," Mavis protested. Their voices grew louder and filled the house.

"What is all di shouting in di house for?" Harry demanded, charging into the living room. "Mi can hear unnu voice all di way in di basement. Doris, wah di matter?"

His wife looked at him and shrugged. Aunt Mavis sucked her teeth and glared at him as she flounced out of the room. Johnny quietly left.

"What a gwaan here?" Harry demanded again.

"Nutten fi trouble yuhself bout," Doris replied.

"All dat shouting was over nutten? Unnu mad or someting? Doris, memba wah ah tell yuh bout you and yuh relatives."

"No bodder start wid dat now. Yuh get di loan from di bank?"

Harry aimlessly switched the channels on the television, ignoring her.

"Well?" Doris pressed him.

"Well what?" he grunted.

"Di bank loan?"

Sinking into the Lazee-Boy chair and adjusting his pillow, Harry sighed, "No."

"No? How come?"

"Don't ask me dat, ask di bank manager," he snapped.

"Yuh nuh haffi bite mi head off."

"What cyan I say? Di bank manager seh we owe too

much on di previous loan and dat is too much risk fi tek wid a young business like ours. Besides, we nuh build up nuff equity pon di house fi use it as collateral."

"So wah dat mean?"

"Dat mean we won't get di money fi improve di restaurant. Dem bank people dem nuh like fi see Black people have anyting fi demself. As long as yuh working fi somebody else nine to five it's okay but try and be self-employed, das when dem try fi keep yuh down."

"Come on, Harry, don't talk like dat."

"Yuh always picking up fi dem white people. When yuh gwine to accept di fact dat white people don't want fi see Black people independent in dis country? Yuh nuh see dis is a racist country?"

"I am sick and tired of people like yuh come yah and blame everyting pon white people every time someting nuh go as unnu want it fi go. Wah if a Black bank manager turn yuh down? Wah yuh have fi seh den, eh?"

"Den mi would haffi seh him was a Uncle Tom."

"Now yuh sound like Mavis. Canada is a land full of opportunities. Wah ever yuh put in is wah yuh gwine get out. A lot of Black people come yah and expect everyting pon a silver platter, while odder people work hard fi wah dem have."

"Yuh stay deh live in yuh dream world. Talking bout Mavis, when she gwine move out of here?"

"Harry, yuh can't expect mi fi put her out in di cold. She is mi sistah and mi wudden like see anyting appen to her."

"She nah work two jobs? Why she cyaan live pon her own?"

"Yuh know she a save fi sponsor her children from Jamaica. She contribute when she cyan."

"God bless di lickle she give yuh fi buy food. She nyam twice dat amount. If she was living anywhere else she would haffi pay rent. One minute is yuh sistah, di next minute is yuh pickney dem. Who next yuh gwine bring in di house?"

"Me cyaan believe wah mi hearing. Mavis, Johnny and Vinette are all staying here whether yuh like it or not."

"Talking bout Vinette, why she haffi give up she place and move back yah?"

"Come on, Harry, yuh know dat it's hard fi Vinette fi pay rent and go to school. Even though mi nuh like she life, she gwine stay here till she graduate."

"Who is wearing di pants in di house, eh?"

"Ah give up mi nursing career fi work inna di restaurant so as fi mek life easier fi di children. After leaving Johnny in Jamaica so long, di least mi cyan do now is give him a chance fi a better life. Mi only wish mi could a did send fi him sooner. Mi nuh like di company Vinette mix up herself wid, but she have ambition and mi gwine help her as much as possible."

Leaving the room, Doris paused at the door to add, "One last ting: nuh bodder show Johnny and Vinette any bad face. Dem is to be treated jus like Karen and Joey, yuh hear?"

"Gwan run up yuh mout, man. Yuh love fi argue too much. Yuh nuh have nutten fi worry bout." Harry turned up the volume on the television.

Mavis had gone downstairs to the basement apartment which she shared with Sheba, still upset with her sister for the comments she had made to her earlier. Mavis had started working two jobs, hoping to save enough money to sponsor Boysie and Sweetie in the event that she became landed. There were times when she wished she had her own place, but she knew that she couldn't afford anything decent. Her boyfriend, Paul, had asked her to come and live with him several times, and each time she had turned him down. Now she thought of reconsidering.

Her thoughts were broken by the sound of footsteps on the stairway. Looking up, she saw Johnny. He came up to her and put his arm around her shoulders.

"I'm sorry fi mek problems between yuh and Mama," he mumbled.

"Don't worry bout dat, man. Yuh know Doris soon cool down. But yuh know she nuh like di Rasta business too much — derefore yuh shouldn't mention bout yuh visit to di ital shop."

"It slip out. But I really like down deh. Iration Dread really irie. A pity him and Sheba nuh deal nuh more."

Coming down the stairs, Sheba said, "Ah hear mi name. Wah unnu talking bout mi seh?"

"Mi was jus talking bout Iration Dread. Mi was at di shop today," Johnny said. "Yuh still check fi di dread though. You two mek a irie couple — " With that, Johnny ran upstairs.

"How yuh feel bout Iration Dread now?" Mavis asked after a slight pause.

"Right now dere are times when ah really miss him,

and den dere are times ah glad him no longer in mi life. But it was nice seeing him today."

"Das natural."

"How about yuh, how tings goin wid Paul?"

"It deh. Although mi care for him, deep dung mi know mi nuh love him. After today, though, mi a consider moving in wid him."

"Wah appen today?"

"Nutten unusual. Me and Doris have one big argument over Johnny."

"Why?"

"Cause him go a Iration shop, and yuh know how she feel bout Rasta. She talk all sorts of tings mi nuh check for. She is mi sistah, and mi love her, but she have a way of saying tings fi hurt yuh feelings."

"Don't I know dat."

"Yuh is her favourite topic around here, especially after yuh give up yuh place and move back in."

"Yuh know how hard it was fi me fi mek dat decision, but mi nevah have nuh choice. It was either dat or continue living wid Iration Dread. And after wah appen mi would a nevah live wid him again."

"Yuh nevah did give me di full bill and receipt."

"Me just couldn't deal wid di whole situation, regardless of how Iration try fi justify it. Ah was being hurt, him wife was being hurt too. Although, Jah know, dere were times I hated her — hated dem both. Like, memba di night mi tell yuh dat him sleep out wid her? Him never say a word — him jus nuh come home."

"Yuh nuh still did mek him move back in again, from wah me hear?"

"It cost too much fi live alone, and yuh nuh know how man stay. Apologies and promises and next ting him move back in again. Di worst mistake of mi life. Pure argument. It only last three weeks dat time. Mi memba after one argument mi spend all night sitting in di park by St. Clair West subway. After dat, mi figure seh it better mi put up wid Mama argument dan wid dis man."

"Why yuh tink mi so hesitant fi move in wid Paul? Mi experience living inna house wid man already inna Jamaica and mi nuh want it yah."

Mavis put her arms around her niece. "Let's face it, Doris bark worse dan she bite."

chapter *seven*

S*everal weeks* after his first trip to Eglinton, Johnny was walking home from school when he saw Marsha and a few of her friends waiting at the bus stop. "Hi princess," he greeted her. "Come yah nah."

"Hi, yourself. I've called you several times, but you're always too busy to talk on the phone. How things going?"

"Yuh know someting? Di only time mi feel at home here is when mi go up on Eglinton to dis ital shop where lots of youths hang out. It belong to dis Rastaman who teach us all sort a tings. Di man crushal."

"Crushal?"

"Mi forget seh yuh a Canadian, yuh nuh know patwah."

"Maybe I don't speak it like you do, but that doesn't mean I don't understand it."

"Yuh safe, man. Mi like yuh jus di way yuh are. Wah yuh doing Saturday night?"

"Nothing much. Probably hanging out at Roller Palace. Why?"

"Yuh waan me and yuh tek in a movie?"

"Don't you like skating anymore?"

"Oh yeah, but ah would prefer someting more private. Mi nuh have nutten gainst yuh friend dem, but mi nuh like too much crowd."

"What do you want to see?"

"Anyting yuh sweet heart desire."

"Okay. I'll check out the movies and give you a call. Here comes the bus. See you Saturday."

"I will be sitting by di phone, waiting pon yuh call."

Later that night, as Johnny lay in bed listening to reggae cassettes Boysie had sent from Jamaica, someone knocked on the door.

"It's open," he yelled turning down the volume on the boom box. Sheba came in. "It seems like yuh having a party in here, man. A which set dat?"

"Studio Seven Hifi. It a tear down Yard now. Boysie send me di tapes dem."

"Nice rhythm. Mek a copy fi mi, all right? By di way, a guy did call fi yuh last night. Did yuh get di message?"

"No. Ah wonder is who?"

"Him seh him know yuh from Jamaica and dat him meet yuh at Iration Dread shop pon Eglinton."

"Mus be Chuckie, from Jones Town. Mi will call him later. So wah a gwaan wid yuh and di dread? Mi notice him a call yuh regular dese days."

"Regular? We talk now and den, but dat's about it. Right now, mi more interested in finishing dis program at Ryerson. Wah bout yuh? Who is dis Marsha who call yuh so often?"

"A girl from school. We go out sometimes but nutten serious. Not right now, anyway. Me and she suppose fi — "

The telephone rang and Aunt Mavis yelled, "Johnny, phone is fi yuh."

"Dat mus be she. Me and she suppose fi tek in a movie tomorrow." Johnny ran down the stairs and grabbed the telephone.

"Hi, Princess."

"Princess? Who is Princess?"

"Oh, a yuh, Chuckie. Mi did a expect another call."

"From Princess?"

"She name Marsha. She and me go school together."

"School?"

"Yuh nuh check fi school?"

"School is fi pickney. Right now, mi inna some bigger runnings, bigger and better dan school. Wah yuh doing tomorrow night?"

"Yuh waan see mi did have a date wid Marsha."

"Di man prefer fi seat in wid a skirt more dan come pon dis business? Wah appen Johnny, di man a get soft pon I? Nuh tell mi Toronto soft yuh up already."

"Just cool, man, mi not soft. Dis is a princess, not a skirt."

"Hear mi, man. Jus tell her dat yuh have another move fi mek. Di more yuh keep she waiting, di more she love yuh. Jus meet me at Bloor subway at nine o'clock. Bigger cousin a go pick us up deh."

"But Chuckie — "

"Forget Marsha, man. Mi a turn yuh pon someting big. See yuh tomorrow night, man."

87

chapter eight

The three sat in a car outside the variety store until the last customer left. "Now's our move," said Chuckie, opening the door. Bigger got out next. The third remained in the car. Pulling out a gun from under his coat, Chuckie pushed open the door to the variety store. "Stick it up, Chiney bwoy! Put all di money in dis bag."

"Move it before ah blast yuh open!" Bigger yelled, also brandishing a gun.

Instead of taking the money from the till, the store-keeper drew out a .38 calibre revolver from under the counter and fired several shots. One hit Bigger in the fore-arm. Chuckie, undaunted, returned fire, hitting the store-keeper in the chest and head. His wife ran in from the storeroom. Seeing her husband sprawled on the ground, she screamed for help.

Panicking, Chuckie pointed the gun at her and grabbed a handful of bills from the till. Bigger stumbled out of the store into the waiting car while Chuckie backed out of the store, his gun still pointed at the woman.

At the apartment they put Bigger to lie on the sofa in the living room. He cried out as they removed his blood-stained shirt, but the wound wasn't as bad as they had thought.

"Take him to di hospital," Chuckie's girlfriend, Heather, ordered.

"Yuh crazy? Yuh waan di whole of Metro's finest come dung on us?" Chuckie snapped.

"Well do someting bout him arm. Ah nuh waan nuh blood pon mi sofa and carpet."

"Jus cool yuhself, man. Yuh nuh see seh di man in pain and all yuh can tink bout is yuh carpet and sofa," said Bigger's cousin Danny.

"No bodder tell me fi cool miself because a mi one gwine haffi clean up dis mess when everyting done. Yuh know how much money mi haffi pay fi dis carpet?"

"Shut up and mek mi tink straight." Chuckie dabbed at Bigger's arm with a towel.

"Danny, who yuh know can look afta bullet wound?"

"Yuh not taking him to di hospital?"

"Like how is only a flesh wound maybe Miss P can look after it. And Miss P cool, man. We gwine haffi give her a smalls fi her trouble, but she all right."

Danny went to the kitchen and dialled Miss P's number. "Hello, is Miss P dere?"

"Who's calling?" said a man's voice.

"Tell her Hyacinth fren, Danny." Danny waited on the line for several minutes.

"Hello, is dis Miss P?"

"Yes, wah yuh waan?"

"Miss P, could yuh come yah and look pon a fren fi me? Him get inna accident similar to Buckie's."

"So how di return go?"

"We'll tek care of dat when yuh reach yah."

"Who is we?" Miss P was cautious.

"Everyting safe, man. It'll be worth yuh while."

"It better. Give me di address. I'll be dere in about an hour."

"Hour too long, man, tings critical round yah," Danny protested.

"If mi seh mi a come, den mi a come."

Danny hung up the receiver and stood by Chuckie in front of the television. "She coming. Wah di news seh?"

"Nutten yet, man."

Heather paced the living room. "When Miss P come, she will see dat Bigger haffi go a hospital," she mumbled to herself.

Bigger moaned, "Chuckie, afta all di plan we mek, mi nevah figure it woulda end up like dis." Chuckie sat staring blankly at the television.

"Chuckie, how much we gwine pay Miss P?" Danny asked. "She nuh work cheap. She nuh mind tek di risk, but she haffi be compensated fi it."

"She a bring everyting?"

"Yeah. Mi tell her fi bring her equipment wid her. She quite suspicious, though. Mi tell her dat we'll fix her up nice."

"We can trust her?"

"Is Miss P or di hospital. We haffi mek sure she keep

her mouth shut — "

The door bell rang. Heather ran to answer the door but found herself blocked by Chuckie and Danny, guns drawn.

Chuckie stood in front of her. "Weh yuh brains deh? Ask who out deh first."

She put her ear to the door and called, "Who is it?"

"Miss P, who else? Open up."

Heather opened the door. A heavy-set woman of medium height stepped in. A short, slim man carrying a large black bag followed closely behind her.

"Me tink yuh did a come by yuhself," said Danny.

"Yuh tink doctor perform operation widout help? Him cool, man. Where's di patient?"

She brushed past him toward Bigger. Her deft movements made it clear that she had done this kind of job before. Within minutes, the wound was neatly bandaged and Bigger asleep.

Miss P snapped her bag shut, washed her hands in the bathroom. She stared at Chuckie. "So how di return go?"

Chuckie stared back. "Wah di damage?"

"Jus pay mi weh yuh tink di job worth to yuh," Miss P said, hands on her hips.

"Wah yuh mean by dat?" Chuckie advanced towards her slowly.

Miss P did not flinch. "Exactly like how it sound."

Danny motioned Chuckie into the kitchen. After a few minutes, they came back. Chuckie handed Miss P a fat envelope. Miss P opened it, flipped through the stack of hundred dollar bills inside, tossed the empty envelope on the floor and tucked the money into her bosom.

At the door she paused. "Di next time — and by di look a tings, dere will be a next time — me expect fi be paid upfront before di work tek place. Mi not even a charge unnu fi housecall, and unnu want come play cat-and-mouse wid mi money. Unnu tink a big bumbo claat woman like me have time fi play wid unnu lickle rass claat bwoy pickney, eeh? Sam, come mek we leave dis rass place before mi lose mi temper."

Sam followed as she went to open the door.

Chuckie moved toward her, his gun drawn. Danny pulled him back.

"Wah yuh doin man? Miss P run tings in dis area. We inna nuff trouble widout tek on more. Cool out, man," Danny advised.

Chuckie slowly put his gun in his waistband and slammed the door. Miss P had belittled him in front of his posse. He swore at her and turned up the television.

Danny went over to sit on the sofa by Bigger and Heather went to her bedroom where Chuckie's son was asleep. She smiled at the baby but looked more desperate than happy and frowned as the baby whimpered, disturbed by the loud laughter in the living room. Heather sucked her teeth and swore at Chuckie and his posse. She went to lie on the bed. Any other time she would have cursed them for making so much noise.

She lay on her side, thinking about the first time she met Chuckie. It was while she was serving time at Vanier prison for trafficking marijuana. Chuckie had come to visit his aunt, also serving time for trafficking. His aunt had introduced them and from then on they had written each other almost every week. He was on the sidewalk, waiting for her, when she walked out of prison.

Once she was settled in her apartment, he had set up a herbs base there, giving her money to support her and her three children. When he was away she ran the business for him. Things had been good for awhile.

The first two robberies were successful. The posse got away and nobody was hurt. When they decided to rob the third store, however, she had made him promise it would be the last. While she didn't mind taking the risk selling herbs, she felt very uneasy risking her freedom for robbery. Now Bigger was lying on her sofa with a bullet wound in his arm and she wished she had tried harder to stop Chuckie.

The thought of going back to prison scared her. When she was in Vanier she had constantly worried about her children, although she knew they were safe with her sister. She had made a vow to spend more time with them. The father of her fifteen-year-old son had been shot and killed in Jamaica several years earlier by a rival gang member. The father of her ten-year-old daughter was serving life in New York for killing a man at a night club.

Heather got up and looked at the baby in the crib. He had Chuckie's eyes, mouth and smile. Since the robberies started she had been having nightmares of police barging through her door and carrying her and Chuckie off to prison. She shuddered. "Life's fucked up," she sighed.

As Doris got up to pour her third cup of coffee, the news came on.

"Two armed Black men held up a variety store in the

St. Clair area tonight. According to the storekeeper's wife, her husband fired, hitting one gunman. The robbers returned fire, wounding the storekeeper in the head and chest."

Doris paused, then sat down again, her empty coffee cup dangling from her hand.

"He was rushed to hospital where he is listed in critical condition. The robbers got away with an undisclosed sum of money. It is believed that they escaped in a getaway car that had been parked in front of the store. It is also believed that a third man drove the getaway car."

Doris turned up the volume on the television. "According to police, violent crime is on the increase in Toronto's Jamaican community. Most Jamaicans are peaceful and hardworking, but police say a fringe element takes pride in — "

The telephone rang. "Johnny, answer di phone and mek mi listen to di rest of di news. Yuh see how dem dutty Rastas a mash up di country. Before dem behave demself like decent people dem haffi come up here and give Black people bad name."

"Doris, yuh cyaan believe everyting yuh hear pon di news," Mavis said.

"Yuh stay deh and defend dem Rastas deh. As far as me is concern — Johnny, who dat on di phone?"

"Jus a school friend of mine, Mama." He picked up the phone and took it with him into the kitchen.

"So Chuckie, wah gwine happen to yuh now? Pon di news dem seh di Chiney man in a critical condition in di hospital. Suppose him dead? Suppose di police track yuh down and charge yuh?" Johnny stammered.

"Jus calm down, man, and stop get bummy. Everyting under control, man. Nobody nuh know nutten bout dis except yuh and di posse. Mi know none of di man dem a bust, but — "

"Don't worry bout me, Chuckie. Yuh cyan depend pon me."

"Yuh better not, else yuh gwine end up six foot deep. Ah keep in touch."

Johnny looked at the dead receiver.

chapter *nine*

A week after the robbery, Iration
Dread stood in front of the oven, laying out patties. The bell
over the door rang. Perplexed by the sudden silence, he
poked his head through the window between the kitchen
and the counter and saw two uniformed policemen, one
Black, the other white, talking to Tuffy and the other men
sitting at one of the tables.

Iration Dread frowned as he recognized two officers
from Thirteen Division who constantly came to the shop. He
had complained to the staff sergeant after the last visit that
their presence was costing him customers. They had not
been back until today. Wiping his hands on his apron, he
crossed through the doorway to the counter area to de-
mand, "Yuh boss nuh tell yuh fi stop harassing mi customers?"

"What's happening, Iration Dread?" the Black one said.

The Rastaman glared. "How much time must I tell yuh
not to call me dat?"

"Isn't that your name?"

"Only wid mi frens. Now to what do ah owe dis visit?"

"We're looking for three young Black men — all are about five-ten, have low afros and are known to frequent these premises," the Black officer explained.

Iration Dread pointed from table to table. "Take yuh pick, officers. Dat description could fit most everyone in di shop."

A man at the back snickered. The officers turned to go. The white officer stopped at a table where a young man sat alone. "Where were you last Saturday?"

"At home, sah."

"And you?" he continued, turning to the boy at the table behind him.

"At home, sah."

"What's dis all bout?" Iration Dread asked furiously.

"What's it to you?" said the white officer.

"I have a right fi know. Dis is fi mi business place dat I am paying taxes for. Yuh tink unnu could come in a white man or Chineyman shop like dis and harass dem customer, eh?"

Iration Dread slammed the counter. "Unnu going to hear from mi lawyer bout dis. Yuh believe seh all Rastas are criminals. It hurt unnu fi see a Rastaman wid a business, eh? Das why unnu come in yah and treat mi patrons like wanted men."

"Just a minute, sir," the Black officer said. "We're conducting an investigation."

"Investigation in to what?"

"We can't disclose that information, sir. Either we

question people here, or they come down to the station with us. We have reason to believe the men we're looking for frequent this shop," the white officer said.

"Wah suspects? Dese are school youths dat stop by fi eat a snack before dem go home. All yuh Thirteen Division bwoys are a bunch of racists."

"Racists?" the Black officer answered. "Suppose someone broke into your store and stole your money at gunpoint, wouldn't you want us to investigate?"

"Jah is mi judge and protector. I and I no need people like unnu fi come to mi assistance."

"Iration Dread, be reasonable — " the Black officer tried again.

The Rastaman exploded. "Don't call I Iration Dread! Do wah unnu haffi do and get di hell out of di place! Unnu driving away mi customers."

"Here's my card. If you've got a complaint, feel free to contact the station. We're here to serve and protect, whether you believe it or not," the white officer said.

"Serve and protect di establishment while trampling on di rights of di poor people. Unnu prefer fi harass innocent people and shoot dung people inna cold blood."

"Mr. Lincoln, we're here on police business. We need to question these men in regard to a case. You know the rules: either they cooperate or we take them down to the station."

Without waiting for the shop owner to reply, the policemen moved toward Tuffy. Iration Dread muttered threats at them, but they ignored him.

He watched helplessly as they led Tuffy and two others

outside to a cruiser parked in front of the shop. Iration Dread felt the tension as each person in the room waited for him to speak. Instead, he went back to the kitchen, cursing Babylon.

Hours later the customers had left the store and Iration Dread and Mikey were getting ready to close up. They heard the doorbell ring. Iration looked up at Sheba. Smiling broadly, he put down the pot he had in his hand and went toward her.

"Irie," he greeted her, holding her hand as he led her to a table. "Di I waan someting fi drink?"

"I thought di store was closed."

"Anyting di I desire, di I cyan get." Iration Dread said softly.

"I'm all right. I heard wah appen today wid di police. Di I all right?"

Iration Dread stroked the palm of her hand gently. "Now dat di I is on yah I feel much better."

Sheba put her hand over his. They sat quietly for several minutes. Clearing his throat, Mikey came forward, "I man gwine trod home now."

Pulling his hand away slowly, Iration Dread got up. "Everyting pack up already, Mikey?"

"Yeah, everyting under control. See di I tomorrow. Sheba."

"Night Ikel," Sheba replied as Mikey closed the door behind him.

Iration Dread locked the store and turning to Sheba, asked, "Di I want a lift home?"

"Sure."

As they sat in the van waiting for the engine to warm up, Iration leaned over and kissed her. She hugged him tightly.

"Let's go over to mi place," he whispered in her ear.

"We haffi straighten out certain tings," Sheba murmured as she caressed his chest.

"We cyan do dat later, all right?"

"All right."

Iration Dread took out a small parcel of herbs and built two spliffs, one for Sheba, the other for himself. They sat in silence, smoking.

Sheba touched his hand lightly. "Di I try di I best. Nutten di I could a do would a prevent di cops from taking away dose brethren."

"I man could a — "

"Could a wah? Di I couldn't do nutten except punch di cops in dem blasted face." Sheba reached for an ashtray.

"Dem would a love dat fi appen so dem could arrest di I. Look how much dem try fi put di I out a business. Di I nevah lose di I temper. No, di I expose dem fi di fraud dem is. Di I justly defend di I rights."

"Wah good dat do fi Tuffy and di odders?" Iration Dread sighed. "Right now, di Beast dem a interrogate dem. Why? Because dem was at di shop."

"Dem could a pick dem up anywhere. Okay, so dem was picked up at di shop, but dat nuh have nutten fi do wid di I."

"It have everyting fi do wid I. Dem was visiting I man. Nuh true?"

"Blaming di I self nah go change di situation. When dem finish questioning dem, dey will be released. I and I know dat dem innocent."

"Is not so simple, Sistah Sheba." Iration Dread looked at her. "I don't know bout di odders, but Tuffy have bout three, four different charges gainst him. Him innocent of dis crime, but wid him record and di pending charges, who knows wah dem will mek him do under force?"

"No one really stand a chance wid di cruelty dat gwaan at Thirteen Division."

"Is not only Thirteen Division. Is at every station."

"So wah I and I gwine do now?"

"If by dis evening dem nuh come forward, I and I will haffi go up deh and find out wah a gwaan."

"I and I should a call Tuffy's babymother and mek her know wah appen."

"I and I gwine wait till dis evening. If him nuh come out by den, I and I will call her. Maybe him come out in di next couple of hours. It nuh mek sense fi worry her fi nutten."

"Iration Dread, di person I most concern bout is di I."

"Nuh worry bout I man. I all right."

"Di I is a great inspiration for everyone dat surround di I. Di I have strengthened all of I and I."

"Jah has strengthened all of I and I," Iration Dread corrected her.

"Okay, but He has given di I a work fi manifest, derefore it's di I duty fi manifest it. Jah don't give anyone more dan dem can bear. He will give di I di strength fi overcome any obstacles. Di I is a strong and positive man. Di I will manage."

Iration Dread looked at her and smiled. He squeezed Sheba's hand.

Some of the members of the posse relaxed in Heather's living room, playing dominoes. Bigger's arm was healing well, thanks to Miss P's regular visits. The money from the robbery had been divided among the posse, with Chuckie getting a larger share. Although the robbery was constantly on the news, there was still no mention of suspects or leads. They felt safe in Heather's apartment.

Bigger and Danny sat around the domino table, waiting for Chuckie to join them. They could hear cooing and giggling coming from the kitchen. Getting impatient, Danny called out, "Wait, man, unnu can't save dat till unnu go to bed? Come play a game of domino, mek me give yuh six love."

"Soon come, man."

Bigger was bored. "Yuh a say dat fi di past hour."

"All right den." Chuckie came out of the kitchen.

"Shuffle di board nuh; mek mi light up mi spliff."

"A who fa herb dat?" Bigger asked.

"Who yuh expect? Iration Dread. Di real McCoy. Him always have good herb, straight from Yard," Chuckie added.

Chuckie took a long pull on the spliff and settled down to the game. They were well into the second round when they heard a loud thud.

The door flew open. Ten policemen, guns drawn, entered. Chuckie and the others were shoved against a wall, then strip-searched. Police threw clothing from drawers onto the ground, pulled the furniture away from the walls, climbed on to counters and checked shelves, cut open the mesh that covered the speaker boxes, and swept the contents of Heather's medicine cabinet into evidence bags. They confiscated small portions of marijuana, but none of the money from the robbery was found.

Chuckie, Danny and Bigger were questioned, then charged with armed robbery and attempted murder. Heather was charged with the possession and trafficking of marijuana. After a few days, all except Chuckie were released on bail. Canadian Immigration wanted him for being in the country illegally.

Sheba lay in bed watching television and enjoying, for the first time in a long time, the quiet of the flat. Shortly after getting the flat her cousin Kingsley had moved in, then Iration Dread had given up his apartment and moved in with them.

There were times she felt suffocated by their presence. Since Kingsley had been working with Iration at the ital shop the men had become very close. Sometimes she would walk along Yonge Street for hours just to avoid being in the tiny flat with the two men. Revelling in her solitude, she thought about the events of the past months. She remembered a fight with Iration Dread, in front of Kingsley. Iration Dread had torn out a handful of her locks. Kingsley pretended nothing happened.

She recalled the time she had come back from New York and Iration Dread had confronted her with a tape she had made several months before. Taking the advice of one of her teachers, she had recorded her thoughts about past relationships and about Iration Dread. During her absence, Iration Dread had searched her belongings, found the tape and listened to it several times. When she came home he had played the tape, and after each sentence, questioned her about it. She had cried throughout.

It was only recently, during Iration Dread's visit to Jamaica, that Sheba had finally decided to give her cousin notice. She was going to rent a house where she could set up a daycare in one section and sublet the rest. Iration Dread could be a tenant. She had also decided to take a year off from her studies to get the daycare started. For the first time in a long while, she was beginning to feel satisfied with her life.

chapter ten

Johnny sat in his room, getting ready to go to a deejay competition downtown. His mother passed the open door, saw him putting on his best shoes and demanded, "Johnny, where yuh goin dis time of di night?"

"To a dance."

"Dance? Where?"

"Up on Eglinton."

"Eglinton? Yuh mean weh dem always a shoot up dance?" his mother shouted.

"Mama, dese are decent people. Nutten gwine appen."

"Yuh nuh have school work fi do?"

"Is a Saturday night. Yuh expect mi fi do school work every day while all mi friends a go out fi enjoy demself?"

"Yuh tink mi tek yuh from Jamaica fi come yah and gallivant all over Toronto? Yuh come here fi mek use of di opportunities."

"Yeah, man, throw everyting in mi face."

Johnny got up to leave. "Mi nevah ask fi come yah. When mi was a child yuh nuh leave mi and come a Canada? Yuh only send fi mi fi ease yuh conscience. Ah was better off wid Granny, at least she care bout mi."

"Yuh ungrateful wretch. Wait till yuh start fi have children of yuh own, den yuh will see weh mi haffi go through."

"Jus leave me alone." Johnny brushed past her.

"Yuh tink mi waan police come knock pon mi door like mi a harbour criminal here? Yuh damn lucky di Chineyman nuh see yuh at di shop — else dem would a haul yuh in like di rest a dem dutty criminals yuh associate wid." Doris began to cry.

"Listen, mi a get outta yah."

"Johnny, please don't go." She grabbed his coat, but he shoved past and headed downstairs, bumping into Mavis who had heard the shouting and had come to placate her sister.

"Doris, let him go nuh. Getting angry won't help di situation."

"Mavis, weh we gwine do wid Johnny?"

"Doris, come sit down. Mi know how yuh feel, but yuh must admit dat him usually stay home. Him jus go from school to di house."

"Did yuh hear wah him seh to me?" Doris sobbed.

"When people get angry dem say anyting. Him nuh mean nutten by it. Johnny is not a bad bwoy. Him won't get inna no trouble."

"But yuh know di kind of dance dem keep up on Eglinton."

"Don't worry bout it, man. Johnny will be all right."

On the train westbound Johnny thought of his mother at home crying. He felt bad. When mi go back home mi gwine tell her how sorry mi is fi di way mi talk to her. Mi nuh waan her fi tink mi ungrateful fi all di tings dat she do fi me.

The train came to a stop at Eglinton West and Johnny jumped off and headed upstairs to the buses. As he was about to board the bus, he saw a woman running toward it. Heather. He hadn't seen her since before the raid at her apartment.

"Wah appen, Heather? Where di dawta a go?"

"Me a go tek in di deejay competition dung di road deh. Give mi a spliff nuh," Heather begged.

"Me nuh deh pon nutten. A di same dance mi a go. Nuff deejays suppose fi deh-deh tonight. Two big set inna one small lawn. When is di last time yuh see Chuckie?"

"Him still deh a jail. Ah use to visit him, but mi stop now. It look like dem a go hold him till him sentence because him nuh have nuh papers dem. Sometimes ah see Bigger, but Danny violate him bail last month so dem throw him back inna jail."

"So yuh still a deal wid Chuckie?"

"Yuh really expect mi fi siddung and wait pon a man till him come from prison? Mi dear, mi have mi life fi live. Anyway, mi suppose fi have a baby soon."

"Yuh lie. Anybody mi know?"

"Yuh memba Rankin? Di guy we did see at di airport?

"Di bad bwoy dat always killing innocent people?"

"Him change a lot. Besides, people always give him bad name fi tings him nevah do. Him suppose fi deejay tonight at di dance. A nuff hit songs him have out, yuh know," she said proudly.

"Yuh really love him, eh?"

"Sure. Him tek good care of me and mi children. Ring di bell nuh. Yuh know how dem bus driver stay — is nuh Jamaica where yuh cyan bawl out, 'one stop driver' and him stop yah."

Johnny left Heather at the dance and walked over to Eglinton to the Tafari Ital shop where he talked with Iration Dread and Mikey as he ate a patty. As he was about to leave, a young Rastafarian youth entered. Iration Dread introduced him as Junior.

"Dem call I man Junior or Jougar. I man have a little set name Jougar Tone Hifi."

"Wah? Di man is a sound man!"

"Not really, jus a likkle house ting. I man jus sit in at di gate, burn two spliffs, listen to some cultural music and read up di Scriptures," Junior replied.

"Dat sound irie. My cousin use fi have a lickle set a Yard — strictly cultural music we deal wid. Ah have a few songs dat mi compose."

"So yuh hear bout di deejay competition dung di road?" Junior asked.

"Das where I going."

The two bid Iration Dread goodbye and walked along Eglinton. After a few blocks, they came to a long, dark alley leading to a basement. Johnny ran down the stairs and to the front, where electronic equipment was pumping out loud reggae music through huge speaker boxes placed in the four corners of the room.

The basement was dark. Only the glow of cigarettes and spliffs could be seen. The operators and several would-be deejays stood around Rankin. The crowd showed its appreciation by banging on the walls; Rankin obviously was the people's choice. After several turns at the microphone, Rankin turned it over to local deejays to entertain the crowd. Johnny finally took the mike and with the encouragement of the others, sang a song he had composed.

After he finished, he went over to Heather, who was standing with a group of women. "Wah yuh tink bout mi song?"

"What song?" She looked upset about something.

"Di song mi jus sing a while ago. Yuh nevah hear it?"

"All right, I guess." Heather shrugged half-heartedly.

"Heather, yuh all right?"

"Dat blasted gal nuh waan come tek way mi man," she blurted out angrily.

"What gal?"

"Dat gal over deh in di red dress," she said, pointing to a woman in the far corner. "Mi hear her seh she deh wid Rankin. Right now, me and mi posse a plan fi buss her ass tonight."

"Be careful, memba seh dat yuh a carry a youth. Mind yuh lose it."

"Mi will be all right, man. Right now, yuh cyaan mek a gal come move in pon yuh territory. Mi haffi discipline her."

"She look like she have nuff friends wid her."

"No matter who she trod wid, mi cyan beat her up."

"Ah wish yuh wouldn't talk like dat. Wah she name?"

"Sandra. Yuh know her?"

"Not really, but mi did see her at di airport talking to mi sistah when she did come pick mi up. Yuh nuh waan someting fi drink?"

"Bring a nice-and-easy fi me."

As Johnny left to get the drink, Rankin came up to Heather. "Who dat yuh was talking to?" he demanded.

"A fren of mine."

"Come go home." Rankin ordered, taking her wrist.

"Wah? And mi just come?" Heather shook him off. "Why mi haffi leave?"

"Don't ask mi no questions, man. Jus go in di car and wait fi mi. Ah waan yuh fi tek cover — a ting gwine go dung."

"Yuh just waan mi fi leave so dat yuh cyan rub up wid yuh woman all night, right?"

"Mi nuh waan nuh backchat from yuh. Yuh hear me? Jus go wait in di car till yuh see mi come." Rankin pushed her toward the door.

"Dis ting yuh talking bout — is another shoot-out?"

Before Rankin could answer, Johnny had returned with the drink.

"Everyting all right?" he asked Heather.

"Wah it to yuh?" Rankin glared at Johnny.

"Nutten. Jus asking."

"Sure, Johnny, everyting's all right. Look, mi will see yuh round." Heather left with Rankin.

Within a few minutes, Rankin had returned. Curious, Johnny watched as he walked up to Spider, the hustler

110

Johnny had met at the airport. Rankin was obviously angry and was making no attempt to hide it. His voice rose.

"Hey bwoy, move out a mi way!" With that, Johnny felt a shove from behind. He was not sure who had spoken or what was happening.

"Who yuh a call bwoy?" came the hot reply.

Gunshots filled the room, seeming to come from all directions. The crowd panicked. Some ran toward the single exit at the top of the stairs, but one of the gunmen had quickly positioned himself there and was firing into the basement to prevent anyone from leaving. Johnny found himself on the floor along with several others. Some of the more resourceful hid themselves behind speaker boxes. What must have been only a few minutes seemed to Johnny like hours. As the sound of sirens drew near, he scrambled to his feet. People fled in all directions.

"Lawd God, a man get shot!" a woman cried out.

"Who get shot?" another woman asked.

"Settle, settle!" a man shouted. "Missa operator, play some music and mek wi nice up di dance."

"Nice up wah? Him no see seh a man dead in di dance?" The woman sounded outraged.

"Mi babyfather dead in di dance," a woman wailed as an ambulance pulled up, followed by several police cruisers.

chapter *eleven*

It was Christmas eve. A group of children were making angels in the snow while others tossed snow balls. High above their heads, a lone Black woman watched them, unseen. Tears flowed down her cheeks.

"... 'Tis the season to be jolly..." She turned down the radio, trying to drown out the song. Mrs. Williams had nothing to be jolly about. From now on, as long as she lived, Christmas would never be the same. Four days ago, the police had come to tell her that her son had been killed by a stray bullet at a basement dance. He was, they said, an innocent bystander in a shoot-out and they had tried to comfort her by promising they would step up their investigations. Mrs. Williams didn't really care about the outcome of the case. It wouldn't bring her son back to her. Nothing would.

She prayed. "Oh Gawd, wah ah do fi deserve dis? Ah faithful to Yuh all mi life and a so Yuh reward mi? Wah kind a God mek Him children suffer like dis?" And she cried.

Once the tears stopped, a wave of fear came over her. "Oh Lawd, mi nevah mean fi seh all dat. Figive me. Ah know why Junior was taken away from me — it was a test a mi faith in Yuh. Yes, das it. Please have mercy pon Junior's soul. Him nuh live a Christian life, but him was a good bwoy."

For the first time since the death of her son, Mrs. Williams began to feel some peace. She thought maybe now she could face it, especially since he would always be in her heart. Tomorrow morning her family and close friends would be coming over to the house, and there were lots of preparations for the funeral. She had to be ready.

Johnny lay on his back in a cell, tears running down his face. It was a year since the shooting. He had been charged and convicted for the death of Junior and sentenced to ten years. Ten years fi wah? Johnny constantly asked himself. One set of newspaper articles claimed he was mixed up in a gang shoot-out over drugs. Other articles said the shooting was over a woman who was involved with rival gang members. As Johnny lay on his bed he asked himself several questions: Did Heather know about the shooting before it happened? Did the argument between Spider and Rankin have anything to do with the shooting? What about the gun used as evidence against him?

A hundred miles away, another man was also lying in bed and thinking about that night. As he played the tape recording of the dance, events came back to him. He smiled as he glanced at a newspaper: "Smith sentenced to ten years." He had escaped another murder charge and he felt good about it. This certainly called for celebration.

He got up from the bed and reached for two champagne glasses. As he poured the champagne, he looked at the woman curled up beside him on the bed. Last night's love-making had been exceptionally good. He smiled. Now, as he sat on the edge of the bed, she woke up and smiled back at him.

"Hi, lover." Sandra took a glass from him and slowly sipped as she read the articles in the Toronto newspapers. She knew why they were celebrating.

Doris sat at the kitchen table, staring listlessly at the blank sheet of paper in front of her. She picked up the pen and began to write.

"Dear Johnny, I left you with Granny to come and start a new life here. I wanted to give you a better future, so I came to a strange country and had to put up with the white people, scrubbing floors, looking after dem pickney and dog. Sometimes I had to work three jobs, morning, noon and night, through di cold winter. The only reason I made it was the thought that one day you would come to Canada and be a part of the family here."

Doris put down the pen and sat for a few minutes. Then she wrote, "I fight night and day with Harry. He never wanted you to come. He said you would make his children do bad things. I begged him to give you a chance. I can't bring myself to tell Granny — if she know, it would surely kill her. All the neighbours chatting me behind my back, saying how my son is a criminal. I am too ashamed to show my face in church. Every day Harry laugh in my face. I always thought you would go to university and be somebody special. But no, instead, you turn out to be a criminal. Why did you have to go to that dance? But you are my son already and regardless of that, I can't just turn my back on you. I love you with all my heart. Your mother."

Doris folded the letter and put it in the envelope. Deep in mi heart, mi know yuh couldn't shoot anyone. Johnny, mi just imagine wah di madda of dat poor bwoy is goin through. Oh Gawd, what have I done to deserve dis? she thought as she sealed the envelope and placed the stamp on it. As she wrote her son's name and the address of the Millhaven Penitentiary, her body shook with sobs.

Throughout the investigation she had held firmly to the belief that everything was a mistake and that Johnny would be freed. Now that he was sentenced, she faced the situation for the first time. Vinette and Mavis visited him regularly in prison, but she did not have the courage to go with them.

Doris slowly got up from her seat and placed the envelope in her handbag. She felt better now that she had written Johnny. She took the Bible and read a few Psalms out loud. She was confident that her prayers would be answered.

Johnny dozed fitfully.

Johnny Smith, I sentence you to ten years in the penitentiary for the death of Junior Williams.

Ten years fi wah? Ah nuh shoot nuhbody.

Yes, he did. I saw him shoot Junior. He start di shooting. It was all his fault.

Heather, yuh lie! Yuh babyfather is di one who start di shooting!

How could yuh, Johnny? Deep in mi heart ah know yuh couldn't shoot anyone, but di police seh —

Di police lie. Oh Mama, why yuh nuh believe me?

I man believe yuh, Johnny. Almost every party shooting dat tek place in dis city, an innocent youth is convicted while di killer is left fi roam di streets. Poor Junior. Yuh know someting, yuh both victims — Junior because him was in di wrong place at di wrong time, and yuh because yuh was convicted by di lies of so-called eyewitnesses.

Iration Dread, yuh always tell us bout di wickedness of Babylon, and now mi come fi realize yuh right all along.

Johnny, ah feel so sorry fi yuh. How could yuh get yuhself mix up in dis mess?

Aunt Mavis, mi miss yuh so much. Wah mi gwine do? Ten years? No!

"Johnny, wake up, man. Yuh having anodder one of yuh nightmares."

Johnny groaned loudly. Sweat ran down his face and soaked his shirt. He rubbed his eyes and turned to get up. "Ras T, is yuh dat?" he mumbled, opening his eyes to find his cellmate standing over him.

"Yeah, man. Who else yuh expect to be here?"

"Ah could a swear dat mi hear voices from di ceiling."

"Who yuh dream bout dis time?"

"All sort of people — mi madda, Aunt Mavis, Iration Dread, Sheba and even Heather."

"Heather?"

"Yeah, man, Chuckie's babymadda — she tell di police all sort of lies pon me fi cover up fi her man, Rankin."

"Yuh nuh know how Babylon quick fi jump to conclusion? Dem nuh care who dem charge as long as dem find someone fi tek di rap."

"Mi sistah a work pon di appeal. She suppose fi visit mi pretty soon."

"Johnny, mi nuh mean fi dampen yuh spirit, but dose tings tek a long time fi come through. Besides, yuh cyaan depend pon dat. Ah hope yuh nuh get false hope."

"I am innocent. Dem cyaan keep mi lock up in yah."

"Tek it easy, man. I know how yuh feel, but getting angry nah go help yuh. Di first ting yuh need fi do is try and get rid of dose nightmares. Dem getting from bad to worse."

"I know, but weh mi cyan do? When is not di shoot-out at di party is di trial. I keep hearing dese voices over and over. Sometimes I feel like mi head gwine split open. Sometimes mi afraid to sleep."

"Ah know. When dem sentence mi couple years ago, mi use fi have bad dreams too."

"How yuh get rid of it?"

"Wah mi start fi do was get up and write down di dream dem. After a while di bad dreams were replaced wid good ones."

"Yeah? Wah kind of good dreams yuh have?"

"Oh, bout swimming on di beach in Jamaica — in Portland, where mi come from, mi use fi go swimming all di time."

"In Kingston we nuh do much swimming, but we still have a good time. Whether I am sleeping or awake, mi tink bout Yard and all di nice times mi used to have den. Inna Jamaica — "

Johnny broke off for a few minutes, remembering Sala.

"Wah yuh was bout fi seh?" Ras T asked curiously.

"Ah was goin seh inna Jamaica someting like dis wudden appen to me but den mi memba bout an incident dat tek place before mi leave — when mi and two of mi friends a come from school and di police arrest Sala, seh him tief a woman money. In front a nuff eye witnesses dem rough him up and tek him dung a station."

"Dem convict him?"

"Him spend a lickle time inna jail before dem release him. Das why ah sure dat when dem find out seh mi innocent dem gwine release mi."

"Dat was Jamaica. Dis is Canada."

"What's di difference? Wah appen to Sala is wah appen to me."

"A true, but tings different yah."

Johnny got up. "Ah nuh waan hear dem negative thoughts deh, man."

Getting up to stand beside him, Ras T said, "Sorry, Johnny. Ah nuh waan offend yuh, but — "

"Fi a Rastaman, yuh negative bad," Johnny sneered.

"I jus a show di man di truth."

"Well, show it to yuhself. Mi nuh waan hear it."

Johnny lay on his bed, his back to Ras T. His cellmate shook his head and returned to his bed. Talking with Johnny had brought back a lot of memories, painful ones he had tried to forget. After three years he was finally past the nightmares that had plagued him for so long. He too had been wrongly convicted. At first he had believed that the fact of his innocence would be enough and that the courts would discover the error and release him. He had long since lost faith in the judicial system. He opened his journal and began writing.

chapter twelve

S_heba got up_ from her cluttered desk and went to stand by the window overlooking the playground. Dressed modestly in a brown skirt and jacket, beige blouse and head-wrap, she looked serious and business-like, without compromising her Rastafarian beliefs. Her troubled face broke into a smile as she watched the children playing below, oblivious to anything other than swings, slides, building blocks and sandboxes.

Sometimes, when she thought about all the obstacles in her life, Sheba wished she were a child again. For the children's sake, she knew she had to continue the battle to keep the daycare going.

"Aren't they just beautiful?" The voice behind her startled her somewhat.

She hadn't seen Akilah, one of the teachers, come into the office. Turning around to face the other woman, she sighed. "Yes, just beautiful."

Akilah could tell something was wrong. In the six

months she had worked at the daycare she had learned to read Sheba's moods. The two women had met years earlier at the Bathurst subway station as Akilah had sat on a bench waiting for Martha, her neighbour. Akilah had seen a Rastafarian woman, briefcase in hand, coming toward her.

"Rastafari, sistah," the woman had addressed Akilah.

"Rasta love, sistah," Akilah had answered, and it wasn't long before the two were sitting beside each other and talking about the lack of services for Rastafarian children.

"For instance," Akilah had begun, "Yuh tink I like fi send Aiesha to dis Babylon daycare, eh? I have to give di daycare people dem strict orders not to give her nutten to eat or drink." She sucked her teeth.

"Each day mi haffi prepare her food and send a snack and a few fruits wid her. One day she come and seh her teacher give her sandwich and milk because she wasn't getting a balanced meal. Mi seh, sistah, I was so mad, I call up di daycare di next day and ask di teacher bout it. I just warn dem bout giving my daughter any junk food."

"Dis daycare ting seem to be a growing problem," Sheba had said. "A lot of Rasta sistah cyaan find suitable daycare fi dem pickney. Either yuh or yuh King man haffi stay home and look after di youth till dem ready fi go to school."

"I cyaan do dat because both I and I King man haffi work and I go to school."

"Wah yuh studying?"

"I am trying to get mi teacher's certificate because I want fi work wid children."

"Really?" Sheba was excited. "I am studying early

childhood education because I want to work wid Rasta sistah like miself fi mek proper daycare fi di pickney dem. Only last night I was reasoning wid another sistah bout setting up a daycare for Rasta children."

"I would definitely be interested in someting like dat now dat I'm nearly finished school."

After that first conversation, Akilah and Sheba had exchanged telephone numbers and promised to reason further about their idea. Now, with other Rasta sistren and brethren, they had set up Jah Children's Daycare. For the first three months or so everything had been fine. Parents paid fees and individuals in the Black and Rastafarian communities gave them donations.

Trouble came when the daycare tried to get a subsidy from the government to cut the costs for the families that used it. To be subsidized, the daycare had to be reorganized. Some of its aims and objectives had to be re-thought and its program changed. This had caused heated debate. Members of the board took opposing sides on the issue. Half of the membership wanted to be totally independent of any government body, while the other half insisted the daycare needed government funds. The debate had dominated almost every monthly board meeting.

"What's di matter, Sheba?"

"Nutten new, I suppose." Shrugging her shoulders, Sheba went to sit behind her desk. Glancing at a letter thrown carelessly aside, she said, "When is not one ting is anodder. Memba dose inspectors dat come last month? Now dem seh we haffi mek repairs to di building."

"But don't dem okay di building already?"

"Yes, but now dem want us to mek more adjustments. According to dem, dem tinking of di children safety."

"Das a bunch of crap."

"Sure it is. We can hardly manage day-to-day, much less find $3,000 for repairs. Since we had to give all di tenants notice yuh know how tight it is round here."

"Wah yuh gwine to do now? Who we know wid $3,000 to lend?"

Sheba straightened her shoulders. "Di only person wid dat kind of money is Iration Dread and I am certainly not goin to him for help."

"Why not? Yuh nuh asking fi yuhself. Besides, look how much time yuh seh yuh help him when him need it."

"Das true and him probably would give it to mi if him have it. However, mi waan tek it to di board first. But wid how tings goin now we might not even have a board by next week."

"Dat bad?"

"Could be worse. After some of dose meetings all I waan to do is to go home and figet everyting, daycare and all. But tinking about di bright faces of di children give mi di strength fi continue."

"Don't worry, everyting will be all right. Yuh jus haffi struggle and try nuh mek tings get yuh down. Yuh strong wid a lot of courage an mi know seh dis is yet anodder battle you will win."

Through the window, Akilah saw the children were no longer in the playground. She got up.

"Is dat di time? I have to go, di children dem waiting. Wah yuh doing later?"

"I might pick up two patties pon Eglinton before I go home."

Akilah laughed. "Yuh sure yuh goin for di patty and nuh di maker? Yuh know yuh and di Dread do mek a good couple."

"Now yuh sound like Johnny." Tears welled up in Sheba's eyes.

Akilah put her arms around her friend's shoulders and hugged her. "How's Johnny doing?"

Sheba wiped the tears away, got up from her desk and stood by the window. "I gwine see him dis weekend. I'm helping him wid di appeal, but das going to tek a long time. Mama tek it very hard, but Iration Dread a comfort me."

"Tell Johnny to hang in deh. So yuh driving home to Pickering tonight?"

"Yeah, after I check Iration Dread at di shop."

"Yuh and Iration Dread getting closer again. Is how long unnu ah deal now?"

"Bwoy, is five years we a bounce, on and off. We have certainly had our share of fights dem and having a third person mix up in it don't help."

"His wife not here dat often, is she?"

"Dat doesn't matter — dey still togedder as a couple. Dere are times when it is lonely living by myself. I always imagine myself marrying and having a family. Di clock is ticking away, yuh know."

"Yuh nuh could have a youth fi Iration Dread? Di youth will always be yours."

"I nevah even tink bout having a youth fi him. I always see him as a married man, not mi babyfather. Right now, mi nah even deal wid no sex argument. I'm waiting fi di right man to come along. And mi madda would probably have a heart attack — she already having a hard nuff time wid Johnny in prison."

"Cho, she would a haffi get over it and tek him or her as her grandpickney regardless of who is di father."

Leaving the room, Akilah added, "By di way, memba to discuss di madda's support group at di next board meeting."

"Tanks fi reminding mi. How is dat coming on?"

"So far, we have bout three women who seh dem coming. Odders will get involved once it get off di ground."

After Akilah left, Sheba thought of what she had said about having a baby for Iration Dread. Although he talked about it constantly, she had never seriously considered it. She focused on the letter on her desk. Where am I going to get $3,000 for repairs? she asked herself.

Sheba looked at the grant forms on her desk and cringed. As director, it was her responsibility to seek funding for the daycare. After deliberating for a few seconds, she decided to work on the proposals at home where she would be more relaxed. She put the forms in her briefcase, turned off the lights in her office and left for the day.

As she drove along the highway toward the ital shop, her mind turned to Johnny and how quickly his life had changed since the day she had picked him up at the airport. She was looking forward to seeing him this week. "I haffi memba to phone Aunt Mavis to see if she still waan to come with me," she muttered out loud as she parked in front of the ital shop.

As she entered the shop, she saw Iration Dread leaving

for the kitchen. He beckoned her to join him there. She hailed the patrons in the shop and followed him.

"Hail up, Sistah Sheba," Mikey greeted her as he wiped sweat from his face.

"Rasta greetings, Ikel. Man, in yah is like a furnace." Pointing to a platter of still steaming patties, she said, "Tell mi das ital stew patties on the tray."

Laughing, Iration Dread handed her a patty on a plate. "Yes, dese are di very same ital stew patties. Sample dem fi mi, nuh."

She bit into a patty. "Mmmm, dis is good. Who bake dese?"

"Ikel baked dem jus a while ago."

"Ikel, di man should get a gold medal for dese."

Grinning sheepishly, Ikel replied, "I man learn from di best teacher. Iration Dread is di master chef round yah."

Sheba finished the patty. "I soundly agree wid dat."

Handing her another patty, Iration Dread said, "Flattery will get di I anyting round yah. So how is Johnny di last time yuh visit him?"

"A one cyan nevah be all right in prison but him finally come to grips wid him situation. At first him was having some terrible nightmares, but now him not so tense like before."

She paused to take another bite, surprised at how hungry she was. "Dem move him from Millhaven to Collins Bay. One is maximum and di odder is medium, but as far as me is concern a prison is a prison." Sighing loudly, Sheba continued. "Iration Dread, I feel so helpless. I wish dere was more I could do fi him."

"How di appeal coming on?"

"Slowly. Di I know how dese tings are. Nuff government tape fi go through while poor Johnny waste him life in prison. Dat reminds me, I have to phone his lawyer. I have been so busy wid di daycare dat I totally forgot."

"How is dat coming on?"

"Today we receive a letter from di building inspector saying dat we have about $3,000 worth of repairs to be done on di building."

"But dem nuh approve di building already?"

"Di I know how dese tings go. Dem will try in every way to keep I and I from achieving anyting fi I self and when I and I are working fi dem, dem tek advantage of us. I haffi find a way of raising money fi keep di daycare functioning."

"When is di next board meeting?"

"Next Monday night."

"Di sistah know dat I man will assist in whatever way possible, but I man nuh have nuh time fi meeting."

"I appreciate di I assistance, Iration, but sometime I wish di I was at di meetings fi see some of di foolishness I haffi put up wid."

Sheba pushed her plate away and continued. "Sometime di board mek mi so angry dat I feel like letting dem operate it demself. Di only reason I don't do dat already is because it's not fair to sacrifice di youth dem."

"Don't let dose problems get di dawta down. Jah call upon di dawta to manifest a work. Jah nuh give no one more dan dem cyan bear. Di I will manage."

"Di I is a good source of inspiration, Iration. Jah call

upon di I to strengthen I and I, when I and I get downhearten."

"Sistren, Jah has given all of I and I strength to carry out I and I works. Seen?"

"Seen, Iration Dread. Each one teach one."

Shortly afterwards, Sheba said goodbye and left for Pickering. Her talk with him had lifted her spirit. Now she felt more confident that things would work out for the daycare. If only Johnny could get his appeal, den I would be happy, she thought as she sped along the highway.

chapter *thirteen*

Johnny sat on a bench, watching other inmates play soccer. Since his transfer to Collins Bay Penitentiary, he had missed his reasoning sessions with Ras T. They had reminded him of the talks he used to have with Iration Dread, and the more he read the books and the Bible Sheba had given him, the more he realized that Rastafari was the way for him. He had so many questions and he wished he could talk to someone who had accepted the faith. There were no Rastafarians in Collins Bay, but there were several Black-consciousness men. It wasn't the same. Sheba had promised to bring him some more books on Black and Rastafarian history. He wondered when she would come.

Johnny felt a tap on his shoulder. Irritated, he looked up. Chuckie and Spider? Johnny was speechless, but Chuckie hugged him and shook his hand. Spider flashed him a smile.

"Wah appen, Chuckie? Spider? Dis must be a dream," Johnny stuttered.

"No dream, man. Here in di flesh," Chuckie replied.
"Since when yuh come yah?"

"Bout a month now, but mi spend most of mi time in di library reading. Unnu was in yah all dis time?"

"Oh yeah. Mi spend a lickle time at Don Jail during di trial, but after di sentencing dem transfer mi straight out yah."

Chuckie had stopped smiling. "Mi hear pon di grapevine bout di shooting pon Eglinton. When mi hear seh a yuh pick up di rap, di first ting mi seh a must frame up, cause yuh and me know seh yuh a nuh killer."

Turning to Spider, Chuckie added, "But Spider, don't yuh did deh at di dance pon Eglinton when dem shoot di youth?"

"Yeah, man. But stop, youthman, a yuh dem convict fi dat murder?"

Johnny nodded in reply. "Chuckie, a nuh Heather your babymadda come give evidence gainst mi — seh a mi start di shooting."

"Heather, who use to be one of mi mules dem?"

"Yeah, man. She same one. Before di shooting she a talk to mi when her man come run her out a di dance. After dat mi nuh even see weh di girl turn and yet she come give evidence gainst mi."

"Mi neva did trust di gal deh. A which man she a deal wid now?" Chuckie sounded bitter.

"Nuh di deejay name Rankin."

"Rankin? Dat tiefin bwoy?"

Spider turned to Chuckie. "Den everybody nuh know seh dat him gun kill di youth. After di bwoy give mi ten weight of herbs and mi pay him fi seven, him a come screw up him ugly face pon mi bout him want him money or else him gwine shoot mi."

"So dat was di argument." Johnny stood up. For the first time, the confusing night leading up to his conviction began to make sense.

"Yeah. Di bwoy jook mi dung wid him .32 and hold on pon mi hand. Mi jus flash him off and pull out mi .45. Mi fire several shots inna di dance," Spider gestured here.

"Along wid nuff odder man. But Jah know, youthman, a nuh mi kill di youth. Everybody know seh a Rankin shot kill him. Even di Beasts dem know dat. But yuh tink dem gwine track a man dung in New York when dem have dem guinea pig right yah in Toronto."

"Ah guess a mi is di guinea pig. So dem did charge yuh too?"

"No, dem nevah charge mi wid nutten bout di dance, but couple months after dat dem tear down mi gates and find mi rings and two weight of herbs. Cho!"

Spider sat down. "Yuh waan see how dem ransack mi gates. Two of dem grab mi and throw mi dung pon di bed. Mi haffi drop some kick and punch pon dem."

He shut his eyes and went on. "Den bout seven odder man gang up and beat mi up. Wid di massive force dem bring to di gates dem did expect a roomful of man and nuff weed and guns. All dem find a jus mi and mi dawta."

"So how much years dem throw dung pon yuh?"

"A fifteen years dem gimme. How much dem give yuh?"

"Ten years fi manslaughter, even though mi nevah fire

a gun in mi life." Johnny felt his chest tighten.

"A twelve years dem gimme fi di robbery of di chineyman shop. Bigger, him turn informer and get eight years while Danny get ten," Chuckie said.

"A one informer come buy herbs from mi and den go call di police dem." Spider spit on the ground in contempt.

"Nuff informer deh a prison yah. Every man a look out fi himself in dis time. Johnny who yuh spar wid in yah?" Chuckie asked.

"Nobody. Mi spend most of mi time in di library reading di books Sheba bring fi mi."

"Sheba a yuh sistah?" Spider smiled.

"Yeah, yuh memba she did introduce us at di airport when mi jus come to Toronto."

"Rahtid! But youthman, yuh get big. A long time mi check fi yuh sistah, but she seh she have a man already. When yuh talk to her again, tell her seh mi still check fi her."

"She suppose fi visit mi soon. Mi can't wait fi get out of dis place. Right now mi just glad fi see somebody mi know in yah." Johnny shook his head. "Loneliness is driving mi crazy."

His arrest and trial had changed him. He knew that. Dark circles had formed under his eyes and his lips were permanently pressed together, ready for more bad news. Now, for the first time in weeks he smiled, remembering Chuckie's crown-and-anchor days in Jones Town.

The soccer game had come to an end and it was time to go. Men filed past them, but they stayed talking by the bench.

"I gwine mek a tracks now," said Johnny, getting ready to leave.

"Hey, wah yuh doin tomorrow, break time?" Chuckie wanted to know.

"Probably reading as usual. Why?"

"Meet me and Spider in di recreation room."

"Sure," Johnny smiled. "Tomorrow." He walked away slowly. Chuckie and Spider stayed behind.

chapter fourteen

Heather stood at the window of her
Regent Park apartment, staring down at the hustlers trying to
sell their goods to passersby. Their wares ranged from
jewellery to clothes, but most of the time they sold ganja.
Often the police chased the men from the corner, but once
they were charged, they were back on the streets again. She
saw a few people she knew, but she didn't feel like socializ-
ing. Lonely, depressed and bored, that was how she felt all
the time now. It frightened her, this listlessness. She took out
a cigarette and lit it on the stove. Usually, she smoked half a
pack; now she was smoking almost two packs a day.

She watched her daughter as she slept in her crib. She
looked like Rankin. This bothered Heather because every
time she looked at her daughter she remembered the pain
that Rankin had caused her. After the birth of their daughter,
she had called him in New York. The woman who answered the phone had told her that Rankin would get back
to her. So far, he hadn't. She didn't mind him having other

women. What hurt her was that he hadn't tried to contact her to find out about the welfare of their child. Her only communication from him was a monthly cheque by post. She knew he had several other babymothers in Toronto, but he wasn't in touch with them either.

Heather heard Ryan, her youngest son, stirring in his bedroom and knew that she should be getting him ready for school, but she didn't feel like moving right now. Her two older children were staying with her sister for a while. Since the birth of the baby she hadn't had a man in her life. She had no interest in the men in the Park. She knew almost all their babymothers.

There was a knock at the door, but she didn't move, hoping that whoever it was would go away. The knocking got louder. She threw on her robe and shuffled to the door. Looking through the peephole she saw her social worker. "Shit," Heather hissed and opened the door.

"You look a mess," said the woman as she brushed past Heather and sat on the sofa in the living room. Taking out her notepad and pen, she settled herself, ready for business.

"I'm sorry. I didn't remember about our appointment today. Let me get dressed."

"Hurry it up, I have to see several other clients in the Park today."

Heather reappeared a few minutes later, trying to compose herself. She apologized again for forgetting her appointment.

"Forget it. You seem to be forgetting a lot of things these days. What's the matter with you?"

"Nothing," Heather mumbled.

"Come on, don't give me that. You know you can talk to me. Of all my clients in the Park, you're the most promising."

"I'm just having a bad day. Everything's getting to me."

"Everything? Like what?"

"This place, the children, always broke, no social life." Heather was surprised to find herself fighting back tears.

"Last month when I saw you, you were excited about starting the training program and getting the children in daycare. What's changed now?"

"I feel so lonely most of the time. It's okay. I'll manage. What do you want to talk to me about today?"

"First of all, I need to find out about the father of your last child, the one you said you were getting support payments from."

"What do you want to know? Every month I declare the support payment, so what's the problem?"

"Declaring it isn't enough. What if he can afford more? That's something we need to find out. Or suppose he decides to stop maintaining his child? That's something we want to avoid. And I've put in a transfer for you to get a house, but there's a long waiting list. It might be a little easier for you to get one in the area."

"Please, I beg you, don't place me in this area. Anywhere, except in Regent Park. I want to get out of here — the place and the people are driving me crazy. I can't take it no more."

"I understand your needs, but it's not up to me, as you know. There're lots of people waiting to move out of the

136

area into larger places, but there just aren't enough vacancies."

"Do you know how difficult it is to live in this area? God!" Heather sighed.

As the social worker got ready to leave, Ryan ran into the living room and yelled, "Mommy, when are we going to eat? I'm hungry."

"Shouldn't he be at school by now?"

"There's no school today," Heather lied, as she ushered him to the kitchen.

"Telephone me with the information about the baby's father. As a matter of fact, come and see me. You have some papers to sign."

"More papers to sign? Didn't I sign some papers already?"

"These are different ones. I need to update your file, especially now that you have a baby."

Heather followed her to the door, fixed a date for their meeting and said goodbye. Since the baby, a lot of things had changed. The strain of taking care of four children without their fathers had become a burden. Family benefits were hardly enough to provide food and shelter for the children. She longed for the life the herb business had provided.

Sheba kicked off her shoes, dropped her briefcase on the coffee table and collapsed on the sofa. She had been at meetings all day and she was tired. The drive from Scarborough to Pickering had seemed longer than usual. Everything was going well at the daycare. She had managed to raise the money for the repairs and she had been getting some encouragement from the government about the subsidy. Akilah's mother support group was getting good backing from the community. Sheba decided to go to bed early and then get up at around dawn to start working on her reports.

She put on her robe, made a cup of tea and settled on the sofa in front of the television. She had hardly sat down when she thought she heard the buzzer ring. No, it couldn't be, she thought. Who would be dropping in on her without calling first? She hated when anyone dropped by without calling, especially when she had work to do. Besides, the only person she knew who lived nearby was a guy from Oshawa. Earlier that day he had said that he might drop by and bring her a spliff. Could it be Anthony? No, he would have called first.

Struggling to get up, she pressed the talk button on the intercom and asked, "Who is it?" No answer.

She pressed the door button, thinking it must be Anthony and that he hadn't heard her.

Sheba yawned and stretched. In a few minutes, she heard a knock at the door. Shuffling over, she called, "Anthony?" No answer.

She opened the door and saw Iration Dread. "Couldn't yuh call before yuh come?" she said in surprise.

"Couldn't di I call before di I come? Wah? You did a expect anodder man? Who di blood claat is Anthony, eh?"

Before she could answer, he had hit her in the mouth. "Why?" she asked him. Another hit to the head.

She ran to her bedroom, but he followed her. He

grabbed a hard-backed book from the table by her bed and hit her in the side. Sheba ran back to the living room, but he followed her again. This time he punched her in the eye and she fell on the sofa. She raised her bent knee against his chest to ward him off. He kneed her in the forehead.

Sheba felt the blows, but they seemed unreal. She was sure she would soon wake up and find herself writing reports. She kept telling herself this couldn't be happening. She crawled to her study and hauled herself onto the bed. It was then that the tears finally came. She didn't hear Iration Dread let himself out.

The next morning, as Sheba winced at her bruises, she wept again. She wondered if Iration Dread was still in the living room and tiptoed down the corridor to peep. It was empty. Locking the door, she picked up the telephone and called the daycare. Akilah answered. Still weeping, she told Akilah why she wouldn't be in.

Akilah was incredulous. "I can't believe him beat yuh up because yuh ask him why him didn't call before him come?"

"I still can't believe it miself, but I have the black eye and weals all over mi body fi prove it. It was like him was a different person. I guess him feel dat I'm his property, so him cyan come whenever and do whatever him feel like."

"He came by here looking for yuh, but I nevah know him would drive all di way to Pickering widout calling yuh first. Him probably checking on yuh fi see if yuh have a man," Akilah said.

"I wish yuh had phoned and told mi dat him was looking for mi. Him foolish fi tink dat mi would keep a man yah."

"But wah if yuh have a man? Him have him woman and him have no intention of leaving her. Him must leave you fi live yuh life. Wah yuh going to do now?"

Sheba's voice shook. "I don't know. I feel numb all over. In di past him have abuse mi, but it's di first time him ever beat mi up like dis."

"An I tell yuh, it will only get worse. Maybe yuh cyan understand better now wah mi situation was wid mi dread. Everytime him beat mi a figure him nuh really mean it and deep down him love mi, but when I catch him in bed wid mi own best friend, ah knew dat was it. I had to get out. Yuh haffi draw di line somewhere, Sheba."

"Mi know. I've given Iration too many chances. Him nah get anodder one."

"Mi understand how difficult it is fi yuh, an mi nuh blame yuh. Many of di brethren and sistren have mi up because mi get divorce and cut off mi locks. Dem nuh understand dat sometimes yuh haffi tek certain steps fi yuh own survival and happiness. Haile Selassie still in I heart, but dere were certain tings I had to reconcile fi I self."

"Akilah, ah could never blame yuh for yuh decision. Sometimes — although is only yuh di I can seh dis to — I and I feel dat being a good Rastafarian is harder fi us sistren dan fi di brethren. Mi just haffi keep asking Jah fi guidance."

Akilah tried to soften the tension. "Mi nuh waan yuh fi start philosophising too much. Next ting yuh hear seh mi is a bad influence."

"Akilah, please." Sheba managed a weak smile.

"Yuh need fi put a piece of tuna leaf on dat black eye.

It will draw down di swelling and get di blood circulating again."

"I don't have any yah."

"When mi come I'll put a piece on it for yuh."

"I'll see yuh later."

Sheba hung up and sat staring into space. She was hungry, but she didn't feel like eating. She winced again as she touched her eye. What was she going to do now? She felt like a child punished for having done something wrong. She decided to write to her sister in Calgary and tell her what had happened. She also decided to get a gun permit, and she vowed she would never take such abuse again.

chapter *fifteen*

ohnny scanned the recreation room for Chuckie and Spider. He spotted them sitting at a table in a far corner of the room, playing dominoes.

"Wah appen, Johnny? Siddung nuh, man. Ah see seh yuh right on time."

"Four man haffi play domino. It's harder fi read di game wid only three man," Johnny said, sitting down.

"A white youth from mi cellblock suppose fi come check me. When him come we can have a real game," said Chuckie.

Spider did not look pleased at the news. "Me no trust no white youth in yah. Dem is all informer," he said.

"Dis white youth cool. Mi check him out already. In yah, it's us gainst di system, whether yuh Black or white. Course, yuh have some racist bastards dat yuh haffi discipline if dem meddle wid yuh," Chuckie said.

Johnny slammed a domino on the table, then turned to Chuckie. "Yuh pass?"

"Pass? It tek better dan yuh fi mek mi pass."

Several minutes into the game Chuckie looked at Johnny. "Johnny, mi and Spider have a lickle move we a work pon fi give us our freedom. Yuh interested?"

"What kind of move?"

"Yuh and I know seh prison life nuh nice and — "

"Me nuh interested in breaking outta prison, if dat is wah yuh mean."

"Listen to me, man. Yuh gwine sit round dis shithole and wait pon yuh appeal or yuh waan yuh freedom now?"

"Sheba talk to a lawyer and him seh dat mi have a good case."

"Bullshit! If yuh have a good case how come dem convict yuh? Listen to me, youthman, ah have been up gainst di system fi years: dere is no such ting as a good case. Di Beast dem know seh yuh innocent yet dem still charge yuh. Di evidence dem bring in di court have more holes dan a sieve yet dem still convict yuh. Look how long yuh a wait pon di appeal."

"Sheba coming today wid di news from di lawyer. She seh ah will get di appeal."

Chuckie snorted and slapped down a domino. "Play yuh hand, man."

Johnny slapped one down. "Di lawyer is getting new evidence. I'll get off man. Ah have to."

"Di only chance yuh have is fi Rankin confess and dat will nevah appen," Spider said.

"Di only solution to yuh problem is fi break out. If yuh tink life is bad now wait till Superintendent Ironheart reach yah. Den yuh see wah prison life bout. Right, Chuckie?"

Chuckie studied the game intently before turning to Spider. "Memba Yankee from Chicago?" he said.

"Yeah man, Yankee was a Black American youth. One time a warden call him 'nigger' and him grab di warden and throw him gainst di wall. Bout ten other guards haffi rush over and pull him off or else him would a kill him. Cho, yuh should a see di warden after Yankee finish wid him. Him face big so," Spider said, drawing with his hands the warden's face.

"Yeah, man, Yankee beat di bwoy to a pulp. Him bruk up him jaw bone, stick him in him eyes and smash him rib cage to pieces."

Johnny shuddered. "Den wah appen?"

"Yuh should a see what Yankee look like after Ironheart and him bwoys finish wid him. Months afterward di youth still cyaan walk," said Chuckie.

Spider leaned back in his chair. "We nevah see him again since dat time."

Chuckie looked at his watch. "Rahtid! Mi haffi step."

As he got up to leave, Spider asked, "Is tonight yuh gwine meet dat guard bwoy?"

"Yep. We haffi go over di plans in more detail. Him is di key to dis breakout."

"Cyan we trust him?"

"Yeah, man. Him all right. Mi have him under control."

Johnny said flatly, "Ah tink unnu crazy fi a try a ting like dat."

"Wah appen to dis lickle bwoy doah, eh? Grow up and be a man."

Johnny stood up. He leaned towards Chuckie, "Who

yuh a call bwoy, bwoy?"

Chuckie reached for Johnny, but Spider stepped between them. "Cho! Di man dem fi behave better dan dis. We haffi have respect and unity fi each man."

"Lickle Johnny is a youth dat — " Chuckie began.

Johnny shoved Spider aside. "No call I lickle Johnny. I man name Menelik. From now on if yuh cyaan call I by I African name nuh call I at all."

"Since when yuh have African name?"

"Listen, man, if di man seh fi call him Menelik, den call him dat. A man's African name is very important to him. Yuh should know dat," Spider said.

"Johnny, er, Menelik know dat mi nuh mean him no disrespect. Look how long we've been friends. Right, Star? It's okay fi mi to call yuh 'Star'?"

"Right, man. We frens from di Yard." They gave the brotherhood handshake.

"Time step up fast, eh?" Chuckie said, "Mi have fi leave now fi meet dat guard. We gonna break outta yah!"

"Yeah man. We gwine break outta yah!" Spider echoed.

Sheba sat in the reception room, waiting patiently for the guard to announce her brother. Several other Blacks waited to see prisoners. As Sheba took out a book to read, a smartly dressed Black woman stormed the glass partition and said something to the guard behind the glass. It was obvious she was angry. Whatever the guard said to her made her even angrier. Muttering a stream of Jamaican curses and ignoring the stares from several people in the room, the woman sucked her teeth loudly and sat down beside Sheba.

"Yuh cyaan mek dose people get to yuh," said Sheba.

Eager for a sympathetic ear, Josephine turned to Sheba. "Yuh know how long mi come and a wait inna dis rass place? Yuh know how much people come after mi and dem get through and gone bout dem business?"

"Ah know wah yuh mean. Is a hour dat dem have mi a wait. Maybe di inmates busy doing someting."

"Nutten like dat. Dem people yah nuh respect nobody else time except dem own. Every time mi come up yah is di same rigmarole. If it wasn't fi Spider mi would a never come up yah."

"Yuh know Spider? Mi bredda tell mi seh him see him and Chuckie in deh sometimes," said Sheba. "Mi know Spider from Toronto a long time ago."

"Who's yuh bredda?"

"Menelik, him use to name Johnny. Yuh know him?"

"No, but a hear Spider talk bout him all di time. Dem convict him fi di murder up on Eglinton."

"It was a frame-up. We trying to appeal di verdict but dem a give us a big fight."

"If yuh need help wid di appeal maybe we can help yuh. I work wid a law firm downtown as a paralegal worker."

"Really?" Sheba replied excitedly. "Tek mi card. When I get back to Toronto I'll come and see yuh."

"Director of Jah Children's Daycare," Josephine read the card out aloud. "Dat sound impressive."

"Don't let di title fool yuh. It's jus a small daycare and I'm head cook and bottle washer."

"Das good. I notice dat yuh on Pharmacy. I'm looking

146

for a daycare for mi son, one close to me."

"Where yuh live?"

"I'm at Leyton, not too far from yuh."

"Come and check out di daycare and we can talk bout di appeal at di same time," Sheba replied.

"Dat sound good. I'll call yuh some time next week."

"See Menelik coming now." Sheba got up. "Tell Spider seh Sheba sends hello," she said.

Sheba watched her brother through the glass partition. It grieved her to see him here, but for his sake she would try to be strong. Picking up the telephone, she said, "Wah appen, Menelik? How yuh doing?"

"Hanging in deh. It look like Iration Dread a tek good care of yuh. What a way yuh get fat!"

"If yuh only knew. Yuh look so thin. Yuh eating properly?"

"Dis is prison, not di Holiday Inn. So what di lawyer seh bout di appeal?" he said.

"Tell mi yuh news first. Yuh get di okay fi get yuh vegetarian meals as yet?"

"Dem seh mi need fi prove dat di vegetarian diet is a part of mi religious belief as a Rasta."

"Das no problem. Ah can get di necessary papers."

"Wah appening pon Eglinton? How's Iration Dread?"

"Him send him love and seh fi stand firm and keep di faith. Him still having problems wid di Beast dem though."

"Ah wish mi could see him, but mi know him naw go come to a place like dis." Sighing loudly, he went on. "Who would want fi come voluntarily to dis dungeon?"

Sheba searched for something to say to raise his spirit.

"Ah finally getting subsidy fi di daycare. Now di parents won't haffi pay so much fi dem children."

"Congratulations!" Menelik pressed his hands against the glass as if to hug her. "When mi free mi will come and work wid yuh. As soon as mi get di appeal mi gwine prove to dem dat mi was innocent all along."

"Menelik —"

"Yeah, Sheba. We gwine fight di system and beat dem."

"Yuh didn't get di appeal. Dem turn yuh dung."

Punching his fist on the table, he yelled, "No!"

"Tek it easy, Menelik."

He stood up and hit the table again. "Tek it easy when I see mi life slipping away in thin air?" he shouted.

"Di lawyer seh — "

"Ah nuh care wah di lawyer seh. Him cyan go to hell wid di judge and di jury and di Beast dem."

"We cyan get anodder lawyer. Mi just meet a paralegal worker who cyan — "

"No more lawyers. Dem all di same. Spider and Chuckie dem right. Mi nah go get nuh freedom on a silver platter. Mi just gwine haffi tek it."

Sheba lowered her voice. "Chuckie? Wah him up to now?"

"Nuh worry bout dem. Dem all right."

"Menelik, stay away from Chuckie and Spider. Dem care fi nobody but demself."

"Dem's no different from di rest of di world. Who care bout me?"

"I and di rest a di family. Iration Dread pray fi yuh every day."

"Me nevah mean fi get angry wid yuh, Sheba."

"Shh. Don't say anodder word. Yuh have a right to be angry. If only — "

He didn't hear the rest. Mi cyaan mek a chance like dis slip through mi fingers. No guards, no more bars, mi freedom.

"What's di matter?"

"Nutten."

"Menelik, yuh hiding someting. What's di matter? Yuh know yuh can trust me."

"Me can't tek dis life no more. Mi haffi get outta yah."

"And yuh will, as soon as we get anodder lawyer — "

"Dere won't be any need fi anodder lawyer."

"Don't yuh dare do what mi tinking."

"How ah cyan tell weh yuh tinking?" He was laughing now.

"Don't play games with me," Sheba said, making her words crisp and formal. "You listen to me carefully, Menelik Tafari. Get that crazy idea out of your head. I'm shocked you'd even think of something like that. Chuckie and Spider are behind this, right?"

He shrugged. "Answer me," Sheba shouted. "Dem no good bwoys encouraging you inna dis foolishness, right?"

"Someting like dat."

"Well, yuh listen to me. Forget it! I know yuh disappointed wid di way tings work out, but tings must get better. We'll win, cause good must overcome evil."

"Sistah Sheba, it's so hard fi keep di faith in yah. If it wasn't for Jah — up to last week I saw a man serving life sentence try fi commit suicide, and yuh know wah? Scared di hell outta me. I feel so — "

149

"Hush, it's all right. Jah Rastafari will always be by yuh side. Always memba dat."

"I can't tek dis nuh more, Sheba."

"Jah nuh give yuh more dan yuh cyan bear. We haffi be strong in dis time. Look, is almost time fi go. See di guards eyeing us."

Sheba picked up her handbag. "Memba what I seh bout Chuckie and Spider? Iration Dread and I are chanting for yuh, and Mama praying in her own way. Try and keep up di faith. Guidance. One love."

"One love, Sheba. Keep in touch."

Sheba watched him being led away back to his cell. She felt drained. On her way out, she saw Josephine standing at the bus stop. Slowing down, she yelled, "Hi there! Need a ride back to Toronto?"

"Tanks a lot. Bwoy, mi couldn't tek anodder bus ride after waiting so long at dat blasted prison."

"Me nevah know bus come all di way out yah."

"Dis is a special bus from Toronto, sponsor by one of dem community programs. Usually ah get a ride, but when ah nuh have none mi come up wid di program."

"Yuh come up often?"

"Once a week. Di law firm I work wid have a lot of clients out yah."

"I'd love to come dat often, but it's impossible. I usually come once a month."

"What's it like running a daycare?"

"Hectic but enjoyable, especially being wid di children."

"Do yuh have any of yuh own?"

"Not yet. Ah still waiting pon Mr. Right."

"Yuh have a long time fi wait, den," Josephine laughed.

"I have a lickle boy. I'm going back to school to study law next year."

"Good for yuh. We need more Black lawyers. I graduated in early childhood education, and I'm thinking of going back to study business administration, but university is so expensive. I have to save some money first."

"I have some money saved up, and I have a few investments."

"I didn't know paralegal workers made so much money."

"They don't. Between yuh and me, I run a herb base."

"Yuh wah?" Sheba looked at the other woman incredulously. "I don't believe it."

"Why not? Cause I'm working for a law firm? Most of mi customers are lawyers and other professionals. Yuh'd be surprised at di amount of people dat smoke herb."

"I cyan imagine. I smoke a spliff now and den when I can get it. When I use fi live wid Iration Dread I use fi smoke more often."

"Iration Dread?"

"Yuh know him?"

"Yeah, I use fi buy herbs from him, but now I import mi own straight from Jamaica."

"Yuh have expensive taste. Yuh must be making lots of money,"

"Money is mi first name and hustling is mi last. Let's leave it like dat."

"Until law school?"

"Until law school."

151

chapter *sixteen*

Menelik sat on a bench, underlining a passage in one of the books Sheba had brought him. He wished he could share what he had learned with somebody inside the prison. At first, he'd written to Ras T in Millhaven, but now that his friend had been transferred back to Toronto for re-trial, he had lost contact with him.

As he turned the page, he saw Chuckie and Spider heading toward him. He pretended not to see them.

"Wah appen, Menelik? Where yuh been hiding?" Spider took a seat beside him on the bench.

Keeping his eyes on the book, Menelik said, "Mi nah hide. I in di library, studying."

Chuckie sat down on the other side of the bench. His upper lip curled in contempt. "Studying what?" he said.

"I tek some courses fi mi grade twelve diploma."

"Yuh gawn a school in dis place? Chuckie laughed. "Yuh must be crazy."

"What's wrong wid goin to school?"

"Hey, don't get mi wrong. I'm not gainst school, but di only school I know is di school of life. I admire yuh fi waan a higher education, but me — survival mean more dan having a diploma."

"Don't need fi go to Babylon school," said Spider. "Mi a herbsman, and me'll always be a herbsman, no matter how many time Babylon sentence me. Wid di herbs dem come wisdom, knowledge and understanding."

"Herbs is di healing of di nation," Chuckie agreed. "So Johnny — Menelik, yuh change yuh mind bout dis move we a mek?"

"Nope. I decide fi keep studying till I get mi appeal."

"Me cyaan believe yuh still hold faith in di system. Not after it fail yuh so many times."

Menelik was firm. "I nuh have nuh faith in di system. I have faith in Jah. Everyone have a cross fi bear and Jah nah give I more dan I cyan manage."

"A true, but Jah also help dose dat help demself," said Spider. "As di children of Israel we haffi fight di evil forces at all times. When Babylon lock us up, Jah give us di power fi overthrow Babylon."

"Wait yah, yuh a seh Jah give us di power fi break outta prison — "

"Yeah, man."

" — and dat by breaking out, we a go overthrow Babylon?"

"Yes I."

"Well, mi nevah tink of it like dat. Anyway, Sheba seh it better fi mi fi stay and fight di system from yah."

"Sheba ever go a prison?" Chuckie cut in.

153

"No."

"Listen to me, man. Figet Sheba. She don't know wah yuh going through in here. Now is di time fi act."

Spider got up. "Memba Shadrach, Meshach and Abednego, when Babylon throw dem in di fire?" he said.

"Dem nevah get burn."

"Dem nevah get burn cause Jah deh-deh fi protect dem."

"So, you a seh Jah a go protect us on dis breakout?"

"Yeah, man. 'Jah is our protector, whom shall I and I fear?'"

Chuckie stood. "Tink about it, man. By tomorrow yuh cyan be free. Free fi do wah yuh want. Yuh nuh haffi tek courses here, man. Yuh cyan go to university."

"Me want fi study law fi defend di innocent gainst di Babylonian system."

"Mi fren, di lawyer. Das great! Yuh mek a good lawyer. As fi me, mi have a score fi settle wid a bwoy in Toronto."

"Yuh only gwine get yuhself inna more trouble."

Leaning over Menelik, Chuckie went on. "No bwoy gwine bus pon mi and get weh wid it. A bwoy haffi be disciplined if him do wrong. Mi shoot him or him shoot me. And if we nuh get outta yah tonight, di dog Ironheart gwine eat us up."

"Me can jus see him face when him hear bout it." Chuckie wrenched his face, then made it go slack.

Spider laughed, "Chuckie, di man should tek up di movies."

Chuckie bowed. "Mi use fi write poetry," said Spider, still laughing. "During school days mi use fi get awards."

"Yuh a poet? Get outta yah." Chuckie laughed, but his eyes were cold.

"I kid yuh not my fren, on dis yuh can depen, all di tings I've said I've done, I did dem all in fun."

Menelik got up and slapped Spider on the back. "Dat was great Spider. Jus great!"

"But now mi cyaan bodder wid di poetry. Di poems can't feed mi youth dem. I haffi deal wid someting dat can tek care a mi family."

"Mi know wah di man mean," said Chuckie. "So Johnny — Menelik, wah bout yuh?"

"Me play di guitar and sing a lickle."

"Sing us a song den."

"Yeah, man, let us chant down Babylon."

"But we nuh have no music."

"We cyan tap di rhythm fi yuh," Chuckie offered.

Chuckie and Spider pounded out the rhythm on the bench. When Menelik had finished, Spider asked, "A yuh compose it?"

"Sure. A very long time ago. I perform it when Rankin dem shoot up di dance." Menelik frowned and looked at the ground.

"Figet it, man. All dat gwine change tonight. Right now, ah haffi mek a move, haffi confirm everyting wid di guard fi tonight. See unnu later," Chuckie said, turning to leave.

Spider nodded. Menelik sat staring at the ground.

"Johnny?"

"Still nuh sure."

Spider sighed. "Nuh sure of wah?"

"Don't get mi wrong. Yuh two is di only frens mi have

in yah. I don't know how mi gwine survive dis prison widout unnu, but it nuh seem right."

"Johnny, ah always defend yuh whenever mi see a bwoy a trouble yuh. Yuh tink mi would mek yuh do someting das wrong?"

Menelik didn't answer.

"Yuh tink mi could a leave mi fren behind inna place like dis while me outside enjoying mi freedom?"

"Menelik, when I and I leave yah wah di I gwine do?" said Spider. "Di I know wah dem do wid innocent, defenceless youth like di I in yah?"

"Yuh mean wah dem do to Lickle D?"

"Yuh got it," said Chuckie. "Every night dem use fi rape and batter Little D till I and di rest a Yardies mek dem back off from him."

"After I and I leave, di I will be on di I own. Di I tink di I cyan manage?" said Spider.

"No."

"Den wah di I gwine do?"

Menelik didn't answer. Chuckie looked at his watch. "Time stepping up. I haffi go now before ah miss di guard bwoy. Spider, yuh know di meeting place. Johnny —" He turned to leave.

"Chuckie, wait."

"Yeah?"

"Ah decide fi come wid unnu."

"All right!" said Chuckie, giving first Spider then Menelik the brotherhood handshake. Spider smiled. "Yeah, man," he said. "Menelik is irie."

chapter seventeen

Chuckie waited outside in the dark.
He shuffled his feet as he looked at his watch. He took a
long drag on his cigarette and inhaled it deeply and looked
at his watch again. He tensed as he heard someone coming
toward him, then recognized Spider. Laughing nervously, he
said, "Wah appen, Spider? Bwoy, me nearly have heart
attack when mi hear yuh coming."

"Who yuh expect?" said Spider. Looking around, he
continued, "So I guess Johnny chicken out pon us after all."

"Give di man time — maybe him jus late. Yuh know
him nervous."

"What time dis ting suppose fi get off di ground?"
Spider paced. "It look like yuh jus smoke a pack a cigarette,"
he said, pointing to the cigarette butts scattered by Chuckie's
feet.

"Man, mi would a rather a spliff, but mi haffi settle fi a
cigarette." Chuckie looked at his watch again. "Johnny late.
What a lickle rass saps."

"It nuh really surprise me. Yuh see how much him was gainst di idea from di start. Maybe him jus panic."

"Oh, figet him, him always was a chicken, even from Jones Town days. Anyway, let's concentrate on dat wall over deh. It a separate us from our freedom."

"Yuh sure dis gwine work?"

"Like clockwork. All we haffi do now is wait pon di guard bwoy fi signal us. Him a leave ropes deh, but him haffi create a distraction fi give us nuff time fi climb di wall and be away in no time."

"And den wah?"

"And den we pick up di car — it have some clothes inside it — mi have it park up couple feet away. Ah know dis girl inna Kingston dat seh mi cyan stay wid her while di heat on — she di one dat arrange di car fi mi."

"Chuckie, everyting depend pon dis one guard bwoy."

"Yuh have a problem wid dat?"

"Tek it easy, man. Ah jus stating a fact. Me only meet him di one time — "

"How come a jus now yuh a bring up dis?"

"Yuh know him better dan me, so ah just assume yuh have everyting under control, but ah get a vibes off him."

"So?" Chuckie's voice was flat.

"So dem di same vibes a get from di bwoy dat bust pon me."

"Him haffi do what him is told, him nuh have no choice. Him in dis too."

"Why him waan risk him job?"

"Man, dis not di time fi start talk like dis. We planning dis ting fi weeks now. Why all dese questions now?"

158

"Is jus a vibes mi have. Maybe it's nutten, but mi is a man dat like fi move off mi vibes."

"Shhh. Yuh see dat?"

"See wah?"

"Di flashing light. Das di signal, man." Chuckie smiled.

"Den let's go, man."

Menelik lay on his back and stared at the ceiling until he fell asleep. Back in Jones Town with Sweetie and Boysie, laughing and having a good time playing dandy-shandy. Granny watches them from her rocking chair on the verandah. She's smiling too.

He finds himself in the Nyah Binghi camp in Bull Bay. Rastafarian brethren, sistren and children chant and praise His Imperial Majesty, Emperor Haile Selassie I. Some brethren are dancing to the beat of the drums. An elder reads a psalm from the Bible. He sits spellbound with Sala and Boysie. The elder beckons Menelik to the tabernacle, "Come," he says and gives him the Bible to read. Menelik looks over at Boysie and Sala. He can see admiration on their faces.

Iration Dread sits behind the counter of the ital shop on Eglinton. The Rastaman has a pleasant smile as he talks with Menelik and the other young men. The door opens and Sheba comes into the shop. Sheba and Iration Dread laugh and talk in the far corner. Two policemen, one Black, the other white, arrive. Angry words between Iration Dread and the police. Menelik and three others are ushered outside to the cruiser parked in front of the shop.

A basement dance on Eglinton. Heather and Sandra

argue over Rankin. Rankin and Spider glare at each other in the dim light. The dub music is loud, and in the shadows Menelik catches bright flashes from the guns. Their smoke mixes with that of cigarettes and spliffs. Some people run screaming, others hide behind huge speaker boxes, others decide it is safer to lie on the floor. A gunman approaches. Menelik tries to run and can't. Instead, he holds his head and screams.

Someone is shaking him roughly.

"Don't shoot mi. Mi nuh do nutten."

Maurice, a Black inmate from Nova Scotia, was standing over him. "Relax man, I'm not gonna shoot you, I just want to talk to you."

"Bwoy man, if yuh only know di dream mi jus have." Menelik stretched.

"You were screaming, 'Don't shoot me,'" his cellmate said. "Anyway, there's something I want to talk to you about. I know that you guys are planning on busting out tonight."

Menelik sat on the edge of his bunk. "How yuh know?"

"Who in the joint doesn't know?" Maurice laughed. "Probably everybody in here thinks about breaking out sometime, so traps get set — "

Maurice wasn't laughing now. " — and you guys are dead meat. Word is somebody high up — you know what I mean — wants to put it to the new superintendent and stir up some shit while he's at it."

"But why use Chuckie and Spider?"

"Nothing personal, could have been anybody."

"How come is jus now yuh seh dis?"

"Didn't know until this afternoon. A guy who works in the cafeteria told his buddy — and news travels."

"Wah bout warning Chuckie and Spider? I suppose fi meet dem tonight."

"Somebody from their cell block said he'd go and warn them, but I don't know if he got to them in time."

Menelik shook his head. "Chuckie was di one wid di plan. Spider, him was getting tired of dis place and him willing fi tek di chance."

"One thing's for sure, you're gonna be glad you didn't go because — "

A siren sounded.

Menelik sat on his bunk, took out his Bible and read a psalm. On the wall was a picture Sheba had given him of His Imperial Majesty seated on a white horse. He stared at the picture for a long time.

Chuckie and Spider ran toward the flashing light, grabbed the ropes dangling from the wall and began to haul themselves up. Boots thumped against the concrete and a loud voice shouted for them to stop.

"Mi rather die trying dan die a coward!" Chuckie shouted back.

"I man haffi conquer Babylon in dis time!" Spider panted but held on to the rope.

The guards fired. As Chuckie fell he could see a guard smiling.

chapter *eighteen*

S*heba sat* on the sofa, staring absently at the letter from Menelik. Her first reaction had been to cry; she had read it three times and hadn't overcome her shock at what it said. Picking up the letter again, she read it aloud.

"Rasta greetings, Sister Sheba. By the time this letter reach you, I'm going to be in solitary — in the hole for thirty days for my part in an attempted breakout by Chuckie and Spider. It breaks my heart to tell you this, Sheba, but Chuckie was killed while trying to get over the wall. Spider's in critical condition after picking up five bullets. I wasn't there when all this was going down, but I was part of planning the breakout. I know this is a shock to you, but try and understand why I decided to go along. But Jah Rastafari stopped me, else I'd be dead or in hospital right now."

"Being in the hole, not seeing or hearing anybody else, is driving me crazy, but just thinking of Jah and what He has done for me gives me the strength to endure this cross. Please don't tell Mama and the rest of the family because it will only cause them more grief. My visitors are cut off, so I won't see you for a long time. Take care of yourself and hail up Iration Dread for me. Tell him I look forward to the day I and I will meet again. Until then, I remain your brother, Menelik."

She sat thinking about her brother until late that night. The telephone rang, jarring her. She looked at the clock, then answered hesitantly. "Hello, is dis Sheba?" A female voice asked.

"Yeah, who is dis?"

"Josephine, man. Sorry to be calling so late, but today was very hectic, and I didn't get a chance to call before now."

"Das okay. I was up anyway. What's up?"

"Yuh hear bout Spider and di odders?"

"Yeah. I got a letter from Menelik dis morning. So how is Spider? Menelik said dat he was in critical condition."

"He's still in pain, but him coming on all right, considering how many bullets him pick up. I'm suppose to go up tomorrow fi visit him — das one of di reason why mi calling yuh. Yuh not going up fi visit Menelik?"

"He's in solitary and cyaan get any visitors right now. When yuh see Spider, tell him I hope he gets better soon."

"He asks for yuh all di time. Always telling me how much him check fi yuh."

Snickering, Sheba said, "Dat Spider still no change since di day I know him. Yuh coming to di mother's support meeting tomorrow night?"

"Yuh know my schedule at di office. If I get off early I will try and come."

"Di meetings were going so good, and all of a sudden most of di mothers stop coming. Now is jus di staff members dere."

"Yuh don't know why?"

"Tell me."

"Rumour has it dat Akilah is a lesbian."

"So?"

"Wah yuh mean, so? Mi know at least three women who seh dem nah come a no meeting run by no sodomite. Dem seh dem nuh mind send dem youth to di daycare, but dem nuh waan fi mix up wid her."

"But mi nuh understand wah being a lesbian haffi do wid her job. Di mere fact dat dem still waan fi send dem youth to di daycare mean dat dem have confidence in her as a worker yah."

"Yeah, but Sheba, yuh know how Jamaicans and dreadlocks dem feel bout dem sodomy business. Man get kill fi dem tings deh. Yuh and me know dat. People really suspicious bout Akilah now, especially since she cut off her locks and divorce her dread."

"But cutting off her locks and divorcing her dread is a totally different ting. If people did only know di amount of time di dread beat her up and bring him woman dem inna di house while she at work. One day she even catch her best friend wid him in bed."

"Is dat why she turn sodomite?"

"Ah cyaan tell yuh — Akilah an me nevah talk bout dat. Dis is di first me hear she might be lesbian. But one thing I do know, she's always been a good friend to me and a excellent worker. Ah mean, mi nevah could did start dis

164

daycare widout her and mi not gwine ask her fi leave cause of a few narrow-minded people. I and I will not judge her relationship. Mek she and Jah work dat out togedder."

"Well, is not everybody tink like yuh, Sheba. But if her dread really beat her up like yuh seh, well — when mi pregnant wid my youth, mi babyfather threaten to kick di baby outta mi. Him grab mi in mi hair and box mi up nuff times in mi face."

"Fi wah?"

"Him overhear mi a talk to a friend pon di phone bout a movie. Inna di movie di police a chase after a man who run in a room weh anodder man a have sex wid a woman. Him only hear di sex part and him start rant and seh imagine mi a talk wid man bout sex and mi pregnant fi him. When him ask mi who di man is, mi figure seh him nuh have no right fi a eavesdrop pon mi conversation, so mi nuh tell him. Besides, him always accuse mi of being wid dis friend."

Remembering when Iration Dread had beaten her up for asking why he hadn't called before coming over, Sheba said, "Sometimes I wonder if dese men have any respect fi dem madda? How would dem feel if a man was beating up dem daughters?"

"When yuh see a man beat dem woman dat way, more time is because dem see dem father abuse dem madda and dem grow up accepting dat as di right way. But mi know nuff man who would nevah put dem hand pon a woman. Dem rather leave dan fight. Before mi forget, yuh know a girl name Heather?"

"Which Heather dat?"

"She have a baby fi Chuckie."

"She's di one dat gave evidence gainst Menelik." Sheba's voice was bitter.

"Dat was when she was dealing wid Rankin. I tink she have a baby fi him. Anyway, Spider asked mi to go and talk to her bout Chuckie. Yuh cyan come wid mi to see her? She live in di Warden Woods area."

"When yuh waan to do dat?" Sheba's heart raced.

"Maybe tomorrow night. Mi gwine call up first and mek she know seh we coming fi check her. All right?"

"But di meeting is tomorrow night."

"Oh yeah. Tell yuh wah, if tomorrow night's okay, I'll come to di meeting and den we cyan go see Heather after. She not dat far from di daycare."

"Das all right. See yuh tomorrow den." Sheba hung up the telephone.

The next day, as Sheba sat at her desk working on a progress report to the board, she heard a knock at the door. She looked up at Akilah and said, "Is it time fi di meeting as yet?"

Handing her an envelope, Akilah said, "I waan to give yuh dis before di meeting."

"Wah it is?"

"Mi resignation from di daycare. I've been offered a job fi work at a women's shelter and mi decide fi tek it."

"Yuh resigning from di daycare?" Sheba was stunned.

"Don't get mi wrong. I really like working wid di kids — and yuh know how much I like working wid di staff yah, especially you — but yuh know mi waan to work wid women, and mi tink it'd be challenging fi work at di shelter.

Besides, it might be better for di madda support group and di daycare."

"Yuh know bout di rumour den?"

"Sure. At first, mi tink di women jus busy and nuh have di time fi come to di meetings, but after a while mi suspect it's because of me."

"But yuh nevah seh a ting to mi." Sheba got up from her desk and stood in front of her friend.

"Ah didn't know how yuh'd react. I know how hard it is fi yuh fi keep di daycare running and fi deal wid di board. I didn't waan to add to yuh problems. Bout di rumours — "

"Akilah, yuh nuh haffi explain a ting to me," Sheba interjected. "We know each other fi a long time, we've worked together on many projects. How yuh choose to live yuh life is fi yuh business an yuh nuh need fi give me or anybody any explanation bout anyting. Though mi gwine miss working wid yuh, mi know yuh'll be good at yuh new job. Wah about di meeting tonight?"

"Das anodder ting. Mi tink we need to cancel di meeting — dere is only one woman confirm so far. Wah we need to do is expand di group fi include maddas from di area, whether dere childen come to di daycare or not."

"Me haffi phone Josephine and tell her dat di meeting cancel," Sheba said, dialling the number.

"Josephine from Leyton?" Akilah asked.

"Yuh know her?"

"Everybody in di area knows her. Every weekend she keep dance in her basement. She also run a herb base dere."

Putting down the telephone, Sheba said, "It look like she leave already. Memba Heather, Chuckie babymadda? We suppose fi go check her and — "

"Am I interrupting?" said Josephine, pushing her head through the open door.

"Come in. We was jus talking bout yuh. Yuh know Akilah, one of our teachers yah?"

"Course mi know Akilah," Josephine laughed. "She's one of mi best customers."

"How yuh doing? I'll leave you two. Dem having a women's rally downtown dat mi waan fi go to. Sheba, I'll see yuh tomorrow. Josephine, dat last draw was boom."

"Is a friend send it up from California fi mi. Is a wicked draw of herbs. Mi smoke di last piece last night. So wah appen to di meeting tonight?"

"Sheba'll tell yuh bout di meeting," Akilah said, as she left the room.

"I'm thirsty, let's go and get some juice. We can talk on di way," Sheba said as she locked the office.

As they drove to Heather's apartment, Josephine called out to several people they passed along the way.

Sheba said, "Yuh seem to have a lot of frens in dis area."

"Not frens, business associates. I get hot stuff from dem when dem can't afford fi pay fi herbs," Josephine said. "Yuh tink mi buy dese expensive clothes and jewellery when mi cyan get dem cheap? Galfren, mi cyaan pay dose store prices."

The car headed north on Warden Avenue. Josephine told Sheba to slow down. "Mek a left pon dat street, das weh Heather live. Come to tink of it, mi use to work fi a dealer pon di third floor before mi start bring in mi own stock. Ah wonder if him still live pon di building?"

Josephine got out of the car and went to ring the buzzer while Sheba tried to find a safe parking place. As Sheba reached the lobby, Josephine said, "It nuh look like she deh yah. Mi a ring di buzzer, but nuhbody not answering."

"Yuh nevah phone her before yuh leave out?"

"Of course, mi call di gal, and she seh she'd be home all day. Mi nuh waan nuh bumbo claat gal come waste mi time," Josephine replied angrily.

As they were about to leave, they saw Heather come in the building.

"Heather!"

"Yeah, sorry I'm late, mi jus run across di daycare fi pick up di baby. Unnu waiting long?" Heather asked as they got on the elevator.

"Bout half a hour," Josephine lied.

Sheba looked at her and shook her head. As soon as they entered the apartment, Heather rushed to the bathroom. Five minutes later she was back. "Bwoy, man, yuh know how long mi a keep up dat piss? One minute more and mi would a wet up miself in di lobby."

"Yuh know a don man name Spragga dat use to live pon di third floor?" Josephine asked.

"Him still live pon di third floor. Yuh know him?" Heather was cautious.

"Yuh mean after all dese years dat no good bwoy no leave from government house and go buy him own? A nuff money him use to mek outta herbs."

169

"Him have a big house inna Jamaica and one out in Brampton. Him only use him apartment as a base."

"Di herb business certainly pay off fi him. A nuff money mi use fi mek fi him, yuh know."

"Yuh use to work fi him?" Heather stared at Josephine's expensive clothes and jewellery.

"Long time ago. Right now mi only work fi miself cause nuff a dem man deh waan yuh fi work fi peanuts while dem bathe inna money, and mi nuh inna dat. So Spragga deh pon anyting now?"

"Yuh mean herbs or crack?" Heather asked.

"Crack? Yuh mean Spragga a touch di shit now? Ah cyaan believe it. Back in di old days dem man used to fight gainst dem kind of ting deh. Now is surprising fi see him start deal wid di shit."

"Mi nuh mind a one hustle off herbs, but mi tink it's disgusting how so much Black people start tek coke and crack. How cyan dem justify selling someting like dat to dem own people?" Sheba glared. "And di saddest ting bout it, a lot of Black women deh pon it."

"Dem man feel seh not enuff money in di herbs nuh more. Crack's easier fi carry and more money involve," said Josephine.

"Dem nuh have nuh conscience? Dem nuh see wah it a do to dem own people?"

"When a one a mek $5,000 in a split second, conscience nuh have nutten fi do wid it. Right, Heather?"

Heather stared at Josephine blankly. After a few seconds, she said, "Yuh know how it go — survival di key in dis time. Sometimes a one don't have nuh choice."

"Everyone have a choice," Sheba retorted. "Mi nuh like fi see people throwing away dere lives like dat. People should — "

They heard a loud knock at the door. Heather got up hurriedly to answer. She spoke softly to the person at the door, and went back to the bathroom. When she came out a few minutes later she said, "Me nuh waan fi rush yuh guys, but mi haffi run a quick errand over to di next building. If unnu want, unnu cyan wait till ah come. Ah won't be long."

"If yuh waan, mi cyan stay wid di baby till yuh come," Sheba offered.

"It's okay, we have to leave now anyway," Josephine said as she ushered Sheba out of the apartment. "As mi already tell yuh before on di phone, dem send Chuckie body dung a Jamaica fi bury."

"Tanks for coming over. Sorry unnu haffi leave so soon. Unnu sure unnu no waan wait till mi come back?"

"Is okay. We have somewhere else fi go," Josephine said, daring Sheba to say otherwise.

As soon as Heather retreated into her apartment, Sheba demanded, "Why yuh do dat?"

"Yuh should tank mi fi getting yuh out so soon," Josephine said as she pressed the elevator button. "Yuh no see di gal string out pon crack."

"Crack?"

"Crack?" Josephine imitated Sheba's voice. "From mi tek one look pon her face mi cyan tell she a snort di shit. Why yuh tink she so spaced out when yuh a preach bout di evils of crack? Yuh see how she hurry to di bathroom after she done talk to di person at di door. Wah kind of errand yuh tink she gwine run to di next building? Ah won't be surprise if Spragga a use her fi deliver him dope fi him, and in return him a give her a piece of di rock fi herself."

Sheba stared at Josephine. "How come yuh know so much about dis?"

"I use to do crack. Five years ago mi look in di mirror and mi see a ghost. I cried. It wasn't easy, but mi clean miself up and mek a vow dat I'll nevah again look like dat ghost in di mirror." Sheba followed the other woman silently to the parked car.

Back in the apartment, Heather took the package Spragga had brought for her and opened it. She made a long line with the crack and then snorted it slowly. She knew the baby was hungry, but only her hit mattered.

chapter *nineteen*

Sheba and Josephine waited in line outside a booze can housed in an old warehouse.

It was a special night for Sheba. After seven years, Menelik had finally been released on parole. This measure of freedom did not satisfy him and he remained intent on proving his innocence, and their time together since his release had been spent settling where he would live and by what means. But tonight was different; Sheba felt that it was a kind of celebration.

As cars pulled up and their passengers scrambled out, the line outside the warehouse grew until at last the doors opened to loud blasts of music. Sheba followed Josephine who pushed her way through the thick crowd.

Behind her two young men argued about the soundclash to come.

"Di only way Soul Connection cyan beat Black Power is if Rankin a deejay tonight," said one.

"Go weh, bwoy, Danny Culture cyan beat Rankin any

day wid di lyrics. Slackness and badness soft to culture right now. Rankin chat too much slackness. Mi nuh like him at all."

"Him only giving di people wah dem waan. Di people waan to hear slackness and das wah him a give dem."

As Sheba edged past a group of men standing in a dark corner, she felt a hand on her shoulder. She turned, startled.

"Wait, Spider, is dat you, man? Who yuh hiding from in di dark?"

Spider laughed. "Sistah Sheba! Why yuh so suspicious of mi?"

"Because yuh always doing suspicious tings. What shady deal yuh now involve in?" Sheba asked.

"I don't do nutten shady. Weh Menelik?"

"Him seh him gwine meet mi yah. Mi tink him would a reach already," Sheba answered.

"Spider, yuh bring di ting fi mi?" Josephine interrupted.

"Outside in di car. When yuh a leave mi will give it to yuh. Ah hope yuh have yuh papers up front."

"How yuh a gwaan so? Look how much tings mi do fi yuh. Yuh mean yuh cyaan give mi some herbs pon consignment?"

"A nuh mine. Yuh know if it was mine yuh nuh haffi ask. Yuh nuh see mi flat pon mi face, mi jus a get off pon mi foot."

"Mi jus a tease yuh. Mi know tings hard wid yuh. Di herbs business mash up. Nuh like first time. Di White Lady tek over di place."

"Mi nuh inna dat. From mi born mi nevah touch crack, and mi nuh intend fi start now. Ah'll tek mi time and build

174

back mi herbs business — look," he said, pointing at a man making his way through the crowd, "see di man yah."

Sheba beckoned her brother to join them. "Menelik, how yuh doing?" Josephine asked.

"Taking di days one by one. Jus trying to pick up di pieces and get on wid mi life."

"I cyan relate to dat," Spider said, taking Sheba's hand. "Come dance wid mi nuh — a long time mi nuh dance wid a real woman, yuh know."

Josephine pushed Sheba toward Spider. "Gwaan, dance wid di man," she said. "Look how long him a check fi yuh." She pulled Menelik toward her. "Come yah Menelik, come mek mi teach yuh di latest dance."

As Sheba and Spider danced, she told him about Menelik's determination to prove his innocence. "Di only way him cyan do dat," said Spider, "is fi Heather tell di police dat a Rankin give her di gun."

"Yuh tink she'd do dat?" Sheba asked.

"I don't know, a long time mi nuh see her. People change over di years — it's worth a try."

"Could yuh go wid mi fi talk wid her?"

"It means so much to yuh?" Spider asked.

Sheba nodded. "Okay, ah'll get in touch wid her," said Spider as he pulled Sheba closer to him. Sheba had never danced with a man other than Iration Dread. At first she tensed as Spider put his arms around her waist, but as he held her gently she relaxed and lay her head on his shoulder. Half an hour later, as Spider left to buy himself a Dragon stout and get an orange juice for Sheba, Josephine came up. "Ah see yuh and Spider lock dung tight. Not even air could a pass through."

"Get outta yah, we jus dancing, das all. Him nuh mi type. Him different from di kind of man mi use to."

"Because him locks not as long as Iration Dread?"

"Dat isn't it. Him smoke cigarette, eat fish and drink beer. Mi nuh deal wid any man dat do dem tings deh."

"Maybe is bout time yuh look at di man fi wah him is and not at him vices. As long as a man don't abuse yuh, ital or low-tal, mi tink yuh should go for it. Mi tink it's bout time yuh move on."

"Yeah, but Spider inna too much shady deal, and yuh know mi always try fi live mi life straight — mi see yuh and mi bredda a dub inna di corner. Yuh memba seh him five years younger dan yuh?" Sheba teased.

"So wah? As long as di man nuh disrespect mi in any way, mi will deal wid him. Him young, fresh and green." Menelik returned and Josephine laughed. "Mi can teach him nuff tings," she said, putting her arms around his neck. Menelik hugged her, then pulled her onto the dance floor. "I'm all yours," he said.

Spider handed Sheba the orange juice, took a bag of herbs from his pocket, rolled a spliff and gave it to her. As Sheba drew in the smoke, she said, "Josephine and I was jus talking bout yuh"

"Really? Wah mi do now?"

"Nutten. Mi was jus saying how different yuh is from di dread dem dat mi know."

"Relax yuhself and enjoy life," he said as he took her

hand. "Yuh might be surprise how much we have in common."

Sheba put her hand under his jacket and felt a gun in a holster. She should have known that Spider wouldn't change much. She looked up at him curiously as they danced and caught a brief smile in the dark.

The music ended and the deejay bellowed, "Bigup all masses and crew from Soul Connection. Jane and Finch masses hold tight. Scarborough posse, yuh LARGE. Bigup di one and only Rankin in di dance. Yuh know a yuh run tings. Come down mi selector and mek we pack up a set tonight." The crowd banged loudly on the walls as the music began again. Sheba tensed. Rankin was heading towards them, followed by Sandra.

"Yuh ready fi mi yet?" Rankin asked.

"Not yet. Mi still have some people fi collect from," Spider answered.

"Listen, man, dis ting a drag out too long. Yuh know how di business go. Mi people waan dem papers now."

"Yuh haffi give mi more time, man. Mi have some of di money, but mi still short. When mi collect from di bwoys mi will square yuh off."

"Yuh tell mi dat yesterday and di day before dat. Right now, yuh a put mi in a bad position wid mi people. Because of dis, dem cut mi off till mi give dem some more papers. Cho! Mi nuh like dem almshouse business yah, yuh know."

"Listen man, mi nuh waan yuh dis mi dem way deh. Cho! Mi tell yuh dat di base a run slow, but tings soon pick up. Yuh haffi give mi more time fi get some papers togedder."

"How much time yuh need?" Rankin demanded.

"Bout a week or two."

"Yuh crazy!" Rankin lowered his voice. "Mi people won't wait dat long. Listen, man, yuh have one more day and das it. If yuh don't come through by den, mi may haffi deal wid di situation differently."

"Wah yuh a do, threaten mi?" Spider stepped closer to Rankin. "Yuh know mi long enough fi know seh no one nuh threaten mi and walk away jus like dat."

"Relax, man. Yuh know di rules."

"Nuh come give mi no bullshit bout rules of di game. Mi give yuh wah mi have now. When mi get di rest of di money togedder yuh will get it."

"Hey, Spider, mi nuh waan yuh tell mi how fi run mi business. Cho! A long time mi know mi suppose fi stop do business wid people like yuh. Yuh know wah, mek mi jus leave before tings get outta hand."

"Hey man, who yuh a talk to dat way?" Spider put his hand under his jacket, but as he advanced toward Rankin, his attention was diverted by loud screams from across the room. Rankin forgot Spider and rushed over to Sandra and Heather. Sandra had pulled a knife from her purse and was about to slash at Heather when Rankin grabbed her hand.

"Jus cool out, man. Nuh bodda gwan wid nutten at di dance tonight."

"Talk to dis gal, yah, if yuh nuh waan nutten happen tonight. Mi stand up yah a mind mi business when she come exalt herself and a run off her mout bout mi mus of yuhself," Rankin shouted, grabbing Heather by the collar.

"Mi waan fi talk to yuh bout yuh daughter. Memba her?" Heather sneered.

"Mi will call yuh sometime tomorrow," Rankin said and walked away.

Heather grabbed at him. "Yuh a seh dat fi di past month now. Mi waan fi talk to yuh now."

"Listen, man, mi nuh have nuh time fi deal wid dat right now. Mi have some business fi tek care of," Rankin said, pushing her away.

"Because of dis gal, yuh don't even have nuh time fi yuh daughter. Every day yuh promise fi come visit her, but all now yuh cyaan reach. Dis dutty gal — "

"Who yuh a call dutty gal?" Sandra grabbed Heather and held the knife inches from her face. "Yuh waan mi poke out yuh eye?" Heather screamed.

"Sandra, give mi di knife, man," said Rankin.

"Get dis gal outta di dance before mi cut her up. As long as she is on yah mi gwine haffi do her someting."

"Gweh. Yuh cyaan do mi nutten, bitch."

"Shut up yuh mout, Heather, and go home," Rankin shouted.

"Mi nah go home till mi talk to yuh bout yuh daughter, yuh wutliss, good-for-nutten rass. From yuh pickney born yuh nevah even fart pon her."

"Hey gal, who yuh a talk to dat way?" Rankin punched Heather in the face.

A tense Menelik watched with Josephine, away from the crowd that had gathered around Rankin and the two women. "Fight a bruk inna di dance!" he heard someone say.

179

A tense Menelik watched with Josephine, away from the crowd that had gathered around Rankin and the two women. "Fight a bruk inna di dance!" he heard someone say.

"It look like two women a fight over a man," another added.

"No, man, yuh nuh see dat is a man a discipline him woman?"

"Cho! Dem must keep dose tings at home and don't carry dem domestic affairs in di dance."

Rankin dragged Heather from the dance. She spat in his face. Rankin kicked her to the ground. As she tried to get up, he kicked her again. It was Spider who held on to Rankin as Sheba and Josephine led Heather outside to her car.

The women drove Heather to her apartment where they put an ice pack on her swollen face. Josephine made her some tea as Sheba tried to comfort her. Hours later, she told them her drug habit made it impossible for her to support herself and her children. Josephine offered to find her a treatment program and Sheba said she would check into other assistance.

"Dis is probably not di time fi talk bout it, but dere is someting mi haffi discuss wid yuh," Sheba began. "It's bout mi bredda's conviction."

"Wah bout it?" Heather was non-commital.

"Look, we both know mi bredda innocent and him conviction base on yuh statement. Him need fi clear him name," Sheba pleaded.

"Wah yuh waan mi fi do?"

"Yuh need fi mek di police know di truth. Yuh have fi mek dem know bout Rankin," Josephine added.

She got up. "Unnu mad or someting? Unnu waan Rankin kill mi? It was him who force mi fi frame Johnny wid di gun in di first place."

"But why Menelik?" said Sheba.

"No reason. Jus appen dat way."

"Jus appen?" Sheba shouted as she stood in front of Heather.

Putting her hand on Sheba's shoulder, Josephine said, "Calm down, Sheba. She — "

"Calm down! She destroy mi bredda's life and it nuh bodder her."

"Rankin threaten fi kill mi if mi nuh go along wid it," Heather said, tears streaming down her face.

"Yuh cyan tell di police di truth," said Josephine.

"Sure. And have Rankin posse come looking fi mi. I'm sorry, mi cyaan do nutten."

"At least talk to mi bredda lawyer and get him advice. Must be some way yuh cyan be protected from Rankin."

"Mi will tink bout it," said Heather. "Look, tanks fi everyting. Mi feeling tired. Ah need some rest."

"All right," Sheba said. "Mi give yuh a call tomorrow, after mi find out if yuh cyan get welfare."

"Ah'll check on di drug rehabilitation programs fi yuh," Josephine added.

"Please tink bout talking to di lawyer," Sheba pleaded as they left the apartment. Heather quickly closed the door.

Back at the dance, the soundclash competition was on. Rankin deejayed, his chants degrading women and glorifying gunmen. The crowd banged the walls, making it clear he was the people's choice. "Turn down di music, police outside," a man shouted, as he ran downstairs. Police soon had everyone against the walls and were searching the building for weapons. Most people were given citations to appear in court, but a few were arrested, including Spider and Menelik. Rankin was gone. Spider and Menelik were questioned then released.

chapter twenty

As **Sheba sat** in the living room watching television, the telephone rang. It was Heather. Sheba and Josephine had gone to her place many times to try to convince her to clear Menelik's name, but she had always refused. Now she was saying she would talk to the police. Whatever it was that had changed her mind didn't matter to Sheba. She hung up, then dialled Josephine's number. Menelik would be at her place and Sheba wanted to tell him the good news.

Josephine answered. "What's up? Yuh sound happy. Yuh decide to accept Spider proposal?"

"Get serious. Tell Menelik dat Heather decide fi mek a statement to di police. She seh she waan fi talk to di lawyer first though. How soon yuh cyan arrange dat?"

"We really busy at di office. Give mi bout a month."

"Das too long. Suppose she change her mind."

"All right, mi will try for a week," Josephine replied. "Pass on di message to Menelik."

"Will do. So when yuh gwine accept Spider proposal?"

"Mi still tinking bout it. Him send over a dozen red roses at di daycare dis morning. Him seh him tinking bout mi."

"Di man a court yuh hard. Galfren, hang on before someone else move in pon him. As for mi, mi a enjoy mi young, fresh and green one."

"Mi cyan see dat. Him don't even come home nuh more. Tell him dat him sistah still alive."

"Wah him get over here him cyan get at yuh apartment?"

Sheba hung up the telephone. A knock at the door announced Spider. "Come in, yuh gwine live long."

"Let mi guess, yuh and Akilah talking bout mi again."

"Wrong. Dis time it was Josephine. Mi was telling her dat Heather decide to talk to di police bout Menelik."

"Mi convince her fi do it."

"Yuh did? Why?"

"Because mi know it will mek yuh happy. Besides she seh she waan move on wid her life. When yuh ready fi talk to her ah'll go wid yuh. Nuff of dat now. Yuh get di flowers mi sen yuh?"

"Yes, tanks. Bout your proposal — "

"Take yuh time. Mi nah pressure yuh."

"Wah if I say no? What den?" Sheba asked.

"Den mi a respect yuh decision. Dat won't stop mi from loving yuh. From di day mi know yuh, yuh have been turning mi down."

"Dat nevah stop yuh from trying." Laughing, Sheba hugged Spider.

A week later, Sheba, Spider and Menelik drove to Heather's apartment to pick her up for her appointment with the lawyer. They were at her door when a white woman from the adjoining apartment opened her door and said, "Tell your friends to stop the noise over there, or I'm going to call the police."

Sheba knocked. No answer. "Heather," she called. "Yuh memba di lawyer appointment today?" she asked. "Heather, open di door. Spider and Josephine dem wid mi. Yuh all right?"

"Go weh," came a faint voice. "Mek mi call yuh later."

Inside, Rankin had Heather by the throat. "Wah dis dem a seh bout di lawyer?"

Heather shook her head. Rankin hit her, and she fell to the floor. He kicked her, then pulled a gun from his waistband and pointed it at her head, "Wah bout di lawyer?"

"Me was gwine tell di lawyer bout di gun yuh give mi fi hide in di apartment after di shooting pon Eglinton."

He hit her with the gun. He pointed it again at her head, then spun around and faced the door as Spider kicked it in.

Spider was on top of him before he could shoot. Heather watched helplessly as the gun went off, hitting Spider in the chest. As Rankin ran for the fire exit, police charged in with guns drawn. Sheba and Menelik followed closely behind.

"Drop the gun or we'll shoot."

Rankin dropped the gun. With hands held high, he slowly turned to face the guns pointed at him. Menelik stood apart. He searched Rankin's face for some sign of fear.

There was nothing there but contempt. From some far away place, Menelik could hear Sheba's sobs as she lay over Spider.

"Is it over?" he finally asked. No one answered.

Glossary

Ah - I

a tru, tru - because

boasty - proud, vain

cho - interjection of anger, impatience, disappointment

crushal - very special, fine, or rough, difficult, hard

cyaan - can't

cyan - can

dandy-shandy - in this context a ball game with three or more people in which one, at the shout 'dandy-shandy', runs out of the line of a thrown ball

das - that

deh - there

deh-deh - was there, were there, is there, are there

dese - these

drape - to stop, take hold of, grab

faada - father

facety (-tiness) - cheeky, impertinent, rudeness

fass - interfering, quick to intrude in someone's business

gawn - gone

Globe and Mail - Canadian National newspaper

gwaan - going on

gweh - go away

gwine - going to

jim skreechie - not upfront, sneaky, illegal business

ku - look, look there

landed - legal immigrant/resident status

lickle - little

lickle more - soon

madda - mother

mi - me, my, I

mout a massy - one who talks too much

nuh - not, an, is, are not, please, won't you, exclamation of affirmation

Nyah Binghi -death to Black and white oppressors. Religous ceremony practiced by Rastafarians, consisting of drumming and chanting. Originating in pre-colonial Africa based on the secret society started by the warrior Queen, Nyah Binghi, they waged guerilla warfare against the European Colonialists. Queen Kitami and Queen Muhumusa pioneered the spread of the Nyah Binghi movement. Although started by women it is now a male-dominated movement.

nyam - eat

obeah - the practice of malignant magic as widely known in Jamaica. The magic is designed or 'worked' upon or on behalf of someone, to be distinguished from Myal which is a curative or healing practice.

rass - the buttocks, often used in an exclamatory way to show strong opposition, scorn, anger, impatience. It is considered very vulgar.

RCMP - Royal Canadian Mounted Police

Talawah - strong

saps - coward, weak of character

smaddy - somebody

sodomite - lesbian

unnu - you (plural)

wah -what

weh - where, which, what, whatever

yah - here